GIRL ON Tour

A KYLIE RYANS NOVEL

Girl on Tour

A KYLIE RYANS NOVEL

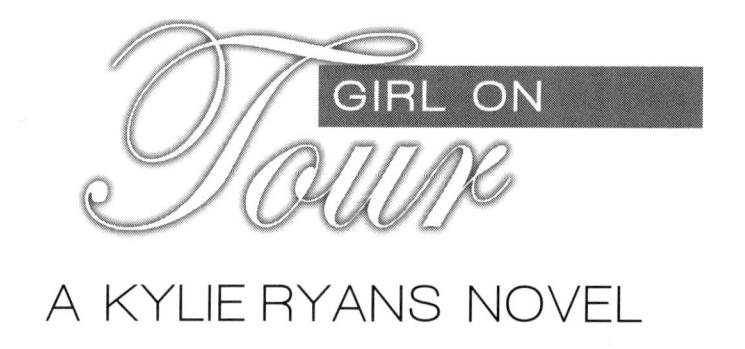

CAISEY QUINN

All rights reserved. No part of this publication may be reproduced or transmitted in any form or by any means, electronic or mechanical, including photocopy, recording, or any information storage and retrieval system, without prior written permission of the publisher, except in the case of brief quotations for reviews. No part of this book may be scanned, uploaded or distributed via the Internet, without the publisher's permission and is a violation of International copyright law and subjects the violator to severe fines and/or imprisonment.

Girl on Tour
Copyright © 2013 by CAISEY QUINN
Cover Design & Layout by E.M. Tippetts Book Designs
www.emtippettsbookdesigns.com
Cover Photo by Lauren Perry of L. Perry Designs
Cover Model: Teale Shawn Murdock
Editor: Mickey Reed

This is a work of fiction. The names, characters, places, and incidents are products of the author's imagination or have been used fictitiously and are not to be construed as real. Any resemblance to persons, living or dead, actual events, locale or organizations is entirely coincidental. The publisher does not have any control over and does not assume any responsibility for author or third-party Web sites or their content.

Published in the United States of America
First publication: August 2013 by Caisey Quinn.
www.caiseyquinnwrites.com

For those of you who feel first and think second. And for everyone who loved Kylie's story and wanted it to continue.

PROLOGUE

The sound of a less than healthy motor cranking up and breaking the sound barrier startled Kylie from the depths of unconsciousness. *What in the world?*

She blinked a few times, dragged her hands across her eyes, and waited for things to come into focus. When they did, she couldn't have fought the grin that spread across her face if her life had depended on it.

She stretched as hard and far as she could, groaning when her back reached its limit. The only thing that could've made the morning better would be if he were still in bed beside her. But she was pretty sure he was responsible for the God-awful noise that had woken her. Yawning, she padded to the kitchen in nothing but his favorite blue plaid button-up. She could smell coffee and the faintest hint of bacon. Hmm, he was a god in the kitchen and a devil in the bedroom. *How did I get so lucky?*

That thought repeated itself when she saw the spread on the kitchen table. Plates of biscuits, sausage, bacon, and fruit waited for her, along with a fresh pot of coffee. Hazelnut—her favorite. Her stomach growled at the sight. She snagged a piece of bacon, thankful that he'd made it crispy just like she liked it. They'd been so busy making love last night she'd never eaten dinner. Pinching off a piece of still-warm biscuit, her mouth watered at the buttery fluffy goodness. *Day-um* the man could cook.

But then she saw something in the window that made her forget all about her stomach. When Trace's shirtless self jumped down off the tractor he'd undoubtedly been working on, it was her hormones that began growling instead.

She dropped the biscuit as if it was poisonous, and her body began to propel itself forward. Towards the door. Until she remembered she hadn't brushed her teeth yet. Kylie yanked open the fridge and grabbed the orange juice. She briefly considered swigging it straight from the carton, but no matter how at home she felt here, she didn't actually *live* here. So she made quick work of grabbing a glass and pouring herself some. After downing it, she walked as briskly as possible towards the door. But it looked awfully hot outside. And she had every intention of helping Trace work up a sweat if he hadn't already. So she filled the glass once more and headed out the door. It slammed behind her and she winced, hoping she hadn't woken Trace's sisters.

If we didn't wake them last night, that probably won't startle anyone. And if the tractor hadn't already jerked them from unconsciousness like it had her, she figured she was safe.

The concrete driveway was scorching so she skittered across it on her tiptoes. When she reached the grass, the bottoms of her bare feet eased onto the coolness of the damp ground. She slowed as she approached the giant contraption Trace was working on. Mostly because he was *bending down* to work on it. Now there was a sight she'd never get tired of.

She figured he hadn't heard her approaching because he uttered a curse as he stood. She watched as he yanked the hat off his head and wiped the sweat from his hairline. His back muscles rippled in a deliberate, satisfying movement that had her heart rate speeding towards a dangerous pace. For a moment she lost her breath. She sipped his juice to wet her mouth so she could speak properly.

"Thirsty?" Kylie called out.

He turned, his hazel eyes bright and clear in the sunlight. "Mornin', sleepy head," he greeted her with his slow, intense grin. The one she knew was reserved for her and her alone.

"Never figured you for an early bird," she said, handing him the orange juice. She watched as he gulped it greedily, the thick knot in his throat bobbing as he swallowed. Overcome by the urge to lick him, his neck, and every other inch of him, she took a step closer. "Sleep well?"

Trace lowered his empty glass and set it on the edge of the tractor seat. "So well it should be a sin," he drawled. He winked and her insides flashed hot. Who was she kidding? *All of her* was hot. And not from the intensity of the Georgia morning sun.

"Guess all that wild sex you stayed up having with that trashy blonde from Oklahoma wore you out. Verdict's in—I'm a harlot." Now she winked and Trace's eyes widened.

He arched a brow and took a step in her direction. "Hmm, that could've been it. Except I didn't see any trashy blondes last night. I saw an amazingly beautiful one. And for the record, that wasn't *wild* sex."

She bit her lip. Okay, he knew a hell of a lot more about sex than she did. But still. "It wasn't?" She fought the urge to pout.

Trace grinned more broadly than she'd ever seen as he gripped her hips and pulled her towards him. "No, ma'am. If you've got some time, I'd be happy to show you my definition of *wild sex*. If you're interested, that is."

Kylie's insides warmed, and she barely resisted the urge to fling herself at him. "Oh, I'm interested."

"Right this way, darlin'," he said as he lifted her from the ground and began walking. Towards the barn.

She squealed, startled by being lifted so swiftly from the earth. "Trace! Where are we going?"

"No backin' out now, Kylie Lou. We've gotta head to Nashville in a few hours. The Trace Corbin tutorial on wild sex starts *now*."

"What about your sisters? What if they—"

"They went out for *brunch* this morning. Whatever the hell that is. Guess they thought we might need some privacy."

"Hmm." She angled her face so she could lick his neck like she'd wanted to. Salty and sweet and all Trace. She grazed her teeth softly against his flesh before pressing her lips to it. "In that case, maybe I'll give *you* a tutorial."

"Them's fightin' words, babe." Trace swung her around so she was facing him. She wrapped her legs firmly around his bare waist. "Hope you can back ' up."

"Only one way to find out, *Mr. Corbin.*"

He growled as he pulled her mouth to his. Those soft lips she loved so much danced against hers, slow and sensuous, then firmer as his velvet tongue sank into her mouth. She felt herself let go as she undulated against him, grinding herself against his warm skin as hard as she could.

He walked them forward, still holding her in mid-air as he pressed her up against the interior wall of the barn. *We're about to do it outside. Up against the barn. Surely that's gotta count as wild sex.*

Wild was exactly how she felt. Wild, crazy, and damn near out of her mind with sheer lust and happiness. She ached to show him just *how* happy he made her. After biting down on his lip until he groaned, she pulled at his neck as if she could pull him any closer. For the first time, she took control. Control of the kissing, control of him. She couldn't get enough. *Nothing will ever be enough with him.* The thought had her panicked and frantic with the need to consume him the way he'd always consumed her.

With her heart pounding, she stiffened so he'd have to let her down. The sound of their panting was all she heard as she fought with his belt until it bent to her will. Her fingers worked deftly to unsnap his button fly. She reached inside the black boxer briefs and wrapped her hand around his thick erection. Lust pooled hot and wet between her thighs. She licked her lips and looked up into his dark gaze. It was wide and on fire.

She let his eyes blaze into hers for a few seconds before she gave him a wicked grin and dropped to her knees.

His gasp of breath was audible. "Kylie." Her name dropped so sweetly from his lips that it emboldened her efforts. She took him in deeper, faster, caressing every inch of him with her tongue as she went. She let her fingernails dig into the firm dips of his hips. His answering groan told her he was enjoying himself. Just as she was finding the rhythm that seemed to elicit the loudest noises from his mouth, strong hands gripped her shoulders firmly, hauling her to her feet.

Lifting her once more, he slammed her roughly into the wall behind them and clamped his mouth down hard on hers. She whimpered, not at the pain, at the force of the pleasure tearing through her. The heady surge of control had awoken something inside of her she'd never experienced before. For the first time, she knew they were equally matched in this area after all. Both of them mindless with need and unaccustomed to giving up control.

"Hold on tight, baby," he rasped in her ear as he let go. She clung to him for dear life, still kissing and licking and sucking at his mouth and neck as he walked them over to a stack of baled straw. In one swift movement he pulled a navy blue blanket from where it sat and tossed it over the straw. She felt his jerky movements beneath her as he worked to get out of his pants and underwear while she was still attached. She grinned against his shoulder.

His eyes never once left hers as he lowered her onto the blanket. He was still staring into her soul with that stormy hazel gaze she loved so much as he sank himself into her warm, wet opening. Fighting the urge to close her eyes, she wrapped her legs tighter around him as he pressed in and pulled out. Desperate for his mouth, she used her elbows to rise up and kiss him once more.

When she let her body relax, Trace's hands moved to her shirt, and she saw the gleam in his eyes. *Holy hell, he's going to rip it right off.*

"Wait," she said, grabbing his hands with hers. "Don't. It's my favorite." She maintained eye contact while unbuttoning it as quickly as she could.

"Mine too," he said softly, right before he finally broke their stare to lower his mouth to her exposed breasts.

There was no fighting the moans that escaped her as he pulled each of her delicate nipples into his mouth. "You feel so good inside, Trace. *Oh God.* It's like—" He cut her off with a hard thrust that shoved an exhalation of pleasure from her throat.

"It's like what, Kylie Lou?"

She shook her head and bit her lip. Part of the reason she didn't finish was because of the intense orgasm about to rip through the center of her. The other part was because of fear. Fear of how he'd react or feel about what she'd come to believe. To know.

It's like you were made for me.

"*Wild* enough for you?" she asked into the stillness when they'd finished and regained the ability to breathe and speak normally.

Trace turned his head towards hers. "I was teasing you earlier. Everything I do with you is wild for me. Slow and sweet, hard and rough, kissing, holding hands, slinging mud, all of it." She would've grinned but his expression was so serious she didn't know what to say. "Babe, I know what the tabloids say. Hell, some of it's true. But I've never done this, any of this—" he paused to wave a hand between them, "with someone I actually gave a damn about. Or even with anyone I didn't give a damn about for that matter."

Now she did grin. "Aww, Trace. You give a damn about me." She placed a chaste kiss on his lips.

He laughed, the deep, sweet timbre of it sending a welcome shiver through her. "Yeah, I do." He kissed her back, a slow brush of his perfect mouth against hers. He gripped her hips suddenly, rougher than she expected.

"You okay?" She pulled back to look into his eyes. The blue and green and gray swirled together in that way it did when he became the most intense version of himself.

"You came back to me. I thought…I didn't think…I—"

She cut him off with a kiss and a promise. "I'll always come back." *No matter how many times you push me away.* She was a junkie. A Trace Corbin addict. And damn proud of it.

Her words lightened his eyes a few shades, and he seemed to be breathing easier against her. "Well, well. Kylie Ryans, if I didn't know better I'd think you were starting to like me."

More like love you. "I guess it's a good thing you know better then."

They'd made love twice that morning. As well as finished their vocals on *The Other Side of Me*, the song that landed Kylie her spot on Vitamin Water's Random Road Trip Tour. A spot she wouldn't have gotten without it, according to her manager. Now she stood with her bags packed in her small studio apartment in Nashville, ready to go back out on the road.

Trace leaned against the counter of the breakfast bar in the kitchen. "You ready, babe?"

No. "Yeah, I guess so." Kylie forced a smile. This was what she'd wanted. What she'd worked her ass off for. Sacrificed everything for. So why did she feel sick about leaving?

That was a list she didn't have time to stand around and make.

After she'd locked up, she took his hand and let him lead her downstairs where a cab sat waiting to drive them to where the tour bus was. Neither of them said much on the way. She wanted to close her eyes and rest, but since her time with him was coming to an end, she used it to memorize his jawline. Her eyes lingered on the thick, muscular ridge in his neck. She grazed her thumb over the smooth skin of the hand that held hers.

When they arrived at the back of the building where the sleek black tour bus was parked, a lump rose unexpectedly in her throat. *It's just a few weeks. Chill.*

Before she could say anything, he was out of the car and around to her side. She cocked a brow as she got out. "You hold doors open now, huh?"

He grinned. "Doin' lots of things I never did before, Kylie Lou."

"Makes two of us."

He didn't let go of her hand until they reached the bus. Trace used both hands to pull her closer. She still wore his blue shirt. *My blue shirt.*

"I sure am gonna miss you, Hothead." Trace kissed her softly on the mouth. She closed her eyes and tried to focus on every single second of it. When he flicked his tongue against her bottom lip, she had to fight back a moan. Lord, the things that man could do with his mouth. She shivered just thinking about it.

"I'll miss you, too. Hey, um, are you going to be okay? I mean, with the label and planning your tour and everything?"

Trace grimaced and she felt stupid for asking. But she was worried, dammit. "Yeah, babe. I'll be fine. Don't waste time worrying about me. Enjoy yourself." He placed a light kiss on her forehead.

"Trace, I didn't mean to—"

"I'm good, babe. It's all good. Get your cute little ass on that bus before I throw you over my shoulder and drag you back to Macon."

Now there was a plan she could get on board with. "I'm going, I'm going." She stood on her tiptoes for one last kiss and a hug. Both ended far too soon. *Like my time with him always does.*

"Behave yourself while I'm gone, Mr. Corbin," she said, playfully smacking him square in the chest even though she was completely serious. *Please don't drink,* she almost added. But she'd seen the dark cloud that had threatened to roll over his features when she asked if he'd be okay.

"I'll try. Long as you promise to come back to me safe and sound, pretty girl," he said, slapping her on the ass as she turned to make her way up the steps of the bus.

"Always." She threw him one last wink before climbing the steps. A lady that looked old enough to be her grandmother sat in the driver's seat staring straight ahead. Kylie greeted her and got nothing but a slight head tilt in response. She missed Carl, Trace's friendly driver, already. Every step she took was like walking deeper into quicksand. Her legs seemed to be completely against the idea of walking *away* from Trace Corbin.

Her eyes began to tear up and she couldn't even see the cool décor inside the bus through the pools of moisture. *Screw this.* She dumped her suitcase in the aisle and sprinted back to the door of the bus.

"Hey," she called out to his retreating figure. Dang, he looked good from the back. *Hate to see you go but I love to watch you leave.*

"Hey yourself," he answered as he turned to face her.

She didn't think. Didn't worry that she might be getting in too deep, moving too fast, or throwing more at him than he could handle. She just did what she was best at. Felt first. Acted on impulse. Once he was close enough, she launched herself into his arms and slammed her mouth down on his.

He caught her, just like she knew he would. His hands gripped her tightly as she wrapped her legs around his waist. His mouth said he was just as hungry for her as she was for him. She deepened the kiss as far as possible, lashing her tongue against his until it ached. When the world began to spin, either because she was falling hopelessly in love or because her brain was seriously deprived of oxygen, she finally pulled back.

Panting, she looked him in the eyes. "I'm going to miss you more than I can even stand. I needed a better goodbye than that."

Trace didn't disappoint. He backed her against the side of the bus, still holding her to him in mid-air. Her mind flashed to their escapade in the barn earlier and she felt the warmth spreading through her core. He ravished her mouth before she could even smile at the memory. When neither of them could take any more, he set her down gently and pulled her in close against his chest. "I'm going to miss you, too, Kylie Lou. So damn much."

Chapter One

Kylie Ryans – Real Life Cinderella Story or Just Another Girl with SDI (Serious Daddy Issues)? By Tammy Paxton

Anyone who hasn't heard that Nashville newcomer Kylie Ryans and fledgling superstar Trace Corbin did more on that tour bus than sleep must be living under a rock. But social media comments indicate that fans are pretty equally divided, torn when it comes to the Oklahoma native's country music star status (starlet or harlot—be honest, how did you vote?) as well as her intentions.

"Kylie would do anything for fame," her estranged stepmother proclaims to anyone who will listen. "She's developed a nasty habit of seducing older men to get what she wants."

An interview with Ms. Ryans' former high school music teacher resulted in a much more heartfelt story.

"Kylie is a tough girl who learned early on that she had a gift for music and that she could use that gift to cope with difficult situations in her life, such as losing her father unexpectedly less than a year ago," Dan Molarity tells *Country Weekly*.

Though both Corbin and Ryans are keeping quiet about their

relationship status and have yet to make it Facebook official, there's no denying that Ryans rode in on the superstar's coattails, joining his tour after being discovered waitressing at the renowned Rum Room. Or maybe she was dragged in on them since Corbin's career has taken a noticeable dive as of late.

Rumors about Capital Letter Records possibly dropping the once platinum album-selling artist have plagued him steadily for the past year. So perhaps this new romance is mutually beneficial for both artists and the media attention will result in higher album sales and concert attendance. Or maybe fans will catch on that they're being played by the publicity machine and boycott both artists altogether.

Relationship status confirmation aside, Corbin, a well-known lover of attractive women and hard liquor, has definitely taken an interest in the previously unheard of Ryans. Reports have surfaced that he even took the stunning young blonde home to Macon to meet his family and friends, which leaves some of us wondering if Corbin has been using, "Hey, there's a spot open on my tour," as a pick-up line or if Ryans is the real deal.

Nineteen-year-old Ryans recently hired publicist Cora Loughlin, (smart move, kid) who only commented so far by saying, "Kylie has the utmost respect for Mr. Corbin. She's extremely thankful to have been a part of his tour. At this time, her primary focus is on her career."

Ryans was recently asked to join Vitamin Water's Random Road Trip tour even though she has yet to commit to a label while Corbin is reportedly in talks to set dates for his *No Apologies* tour. The only way to determine whether or not Ryans has the chops to make it in Nashville is to see her perform, and once you do, you'll likely agree that she's more than a flash in the pan. However, the question remains: is there a real romance brewing between Corbin and Ryans, or is this just a case of a young woman working out her daddy issues with a more than willing participant? Only time will tell. Well, time and maybe Twitter. –TAMMY PAXTON

"*Have* you seen it?" Kylie screeched at her boyfriend via Skype.

"Yeah, Kylie Lou. I read it as soon as I got your text," his pixelated image told her. "But I mean, so what? We knew they would talk." Trace shrugged his shoulders and glanced down at what she knew was probably his iPhone in his hand.

"She said I have 'daddy issues', Trace, like I'm using you or something. And the woman talked to freaking Darla of all people." Kylie leaned back in the tight booth on the bus, wishing she could reach out and let him put his arms around her. But she couldn't, so she folded her arms across her chest, knowing it wasn't attractive to pout but unable to help herself.

"Babe, it's not as bad as you think." He looked up and his warm hazel eyes stared into hers. "Actually, Tammy did a decent job of presenting both sides, and she was honest for the most part. You know how it looks. There's not a whole lot about us that makes sense."

Ouch, she thought to herself as she flinched back from his comment. "Oh-kay. So you want to just forget the whole thing now? Save ourselves the trouble of figuring out what everyone else obviously already knows?" *Please say no.*

"Easy, Hothead," her boyfriend said with a grin. "If one little article sends you running for the hills, I'm not sure I believe you're committed to this long-distance dating thing."

She frowned, though she was barely containing the grin his words elicited. "You know I am. But my God, why is any of this anyone's business?" She still couldn't figure out why people cared what she did or what she ate for breakfast or whatever. No one back home in Pride, Oklahoma, had ever paid any attention to her, online or otherwise. Now that she was linked to Trace, even though it was mostly by unconfirmed rumors, she was suddenly a topic of interest.

"You remember that day on the bus—the day you met Cora?" Trace asked as he snuck another glance at his phone.

"Yeah, and speaking of Cora, I've been meaning to ask—"

"No, we didn't," Trace cut her off, shaking his head. "Focus, Kylie. Remember what I said about having a thick skin?"

"Yeah, superhuman thick. I remember," she told him, leaning closer towards the MacBook screen. "I thought you were an ass but I was actually listening, believe it or not."

"Well, now you know I'm an ass." He winked but then his expression was serious. "But I'm glad you were listening because this is what I was talking about. Don't stress about *what* they say. Just be glad they're talking about you, period. Look at it as free publicity."

"Trace—" She began to argue but her own phone buzzed on the table next to the computer. She glanced at the screen. A handsome face behind rectangular black frames appeared. "Um, it's Chaz."

"Yeah, hey, I gotta get off here anyways. I need to call the guys back about this tour. Mike says hi, by the way." At the mention of his flirty bass player, Trace rolled his eyes but kept going. "Don't stress. Get some sleep on the way to Phoenix. Miss you, babe," he said in a rush.

"Miss you, too."

And then he was gone. Kylie closed the chat window and answered her phone. "Hey there most awesomest, hardest working, handsomest manager ever," she greeted her caller.

"Hello, gorgeous," he responded. "So is Tammy Paxton a bitch or what?"

Kylie's gaze fell on the *Country Weekly* webpage still open on her computer screen. "Ugh, I know, right? Trace didn't think it was a big deal but the daddy issues thing was low."

"Yeah it was," her manager agreed enthusiastically. *See, he gets it*. She was extremely glad that he was still her manager. She'd almost lost him when she let her emotions get the better of her. Trace hadn't nicknamed her "Hothead" for nothing. "So I'm calling because I have news."

"About the cute guy from dinner last night? The one you have a picture of on your Facebook?"

"No. *That* news is none of your business, my dear," he snapped with false snark.

"Yeah, well, don't cut a country music album because then it will be everyone's business," Kylie informed him.

"'Kay, I'll check that off my list of things to do then. Listen, so I know you're probably enjoying having that big luxurious bus all to yourself right now but Lily Taite should be there within the hour so you can get going to Phoenix, and um…there's been a last minute change."

Lily Taite was Trace's younger sister Rae's age and had a rich daddy who'd paid for her album of whiny break up songs and probably her spot on the tour. She also dotted the Is in her name with pink hearts. Kylie wasn't really all that enthusiastic about touring with her, but it was Chaz's tone when he'd brought up the last minute change that made her nervous.

"What kind of change?"

"Lauryn McCray backed out…and rumors are spreading that she's pregnant."

Kylie was floored. Lauryn McCray was only a couple years older than her and had already written with some of country music's biggest stars. Kylie had been super excited to work with her. And now she was pregnant? She stared blankly at Chaz's image on her phone. He was clearly waiting for her to respond. "What?" Oh crap. That meant she and Princess Lily would be all alone. Awesome.

"Yeah, so the Vitamin Water people had a few backups on standby and they chose one. She should be there any minute." She opened her mouth to ask who but her manager rushed on. "I'm sorry I couldn't tell you sooner. I was on another call and just got their message about the situation."

Okay, well that was good news as far as she was concerned. So why did he seem so stressed out about it? "So who's going to be the third girl then?" she asked into the phone.

"I am," said an auburn-haired figure ascending the steps to the bus. "But just because I was added late doesn't mean you get top billing over me or anything."

"I'll call you back, Chaz," Kylie murmured before ending the call.

"Mia Montgomery," the tall, slender woman said, tossing Kylie a smirk as she held out her hand. "I don't think we've officially met."

CHAPTER Two

"Yeah, um, no, we haven't," Kylie stuttered as she struggled to wrangle herself out of the booth and to her feet.

She stood in front of Mia, unsure as to whether she should shake the girl's hand and formally introduce herself or just say to hell with the pretense and ask about her relationship with Trace.

"Not really all that articulate unless you're singing, huh?" Mia surmised out loud.

With brows arched in surprise at the forward question, Kylie clenched her fists and fought the sudden urge to fidget. Unable to put her finger on what it was exactly that bothered her so much about the girl, she decided to forego an introduction. Clearly they knew who the other was.

"So I already put my stuff in the front bedroom," Kylie informed her while gesturing towards the back of the bus. "The middle suite is the biggest. If you want to snag it before Lily you should probably put your stuff in there now before she gets here."

Dark green eyes widened slightly as Mia's forehead wrinkled. *Well good. At least she's as put off by me as I am by her*, Kylie thought. "You didn't want the suite?" Mia asked, looking mildly confused and majorly wary.

"Nah. I don't have much stuff so no point in all that space."

Mia narrowed her eyes as if she suspected this was a trap. "Okay. Well, I'm going to go unpack then."

"Okay." Kylie waited to see if there was anything further, but the other woman turned her back, tossing her hair behind her as she went.

Once she was out of sight, Kylie slid back into the booth and rubbed her temples. *This should be interesting. And miserable.* A heaviness settled onto her chest. She missed Trace like hell already.

Lily was an hour late, which meant the girls arrived in Phoenix an hour behind schedule. It also meant that the two hours Kylie had spent waiting on the bus could've been spent with Trace. Both facts left her more than a little annoyed.

Where Mia was quiet and seemed to be silently judging everyone, Lily Taite was oblivious. To pretty much everything. And she hadn't stopped yammering since she stepped on the bus the night before.

Kylie had just woken up and stumbled into the cramped kitchen area to make coffee. Already Lily Taite was keeping up a steady stream of chatter. "So my dad like totally promised I was getting the master suite on the bus, but I guess you guys decided to do a first-come-first-serve thing and that's cool," the tiny blonde chirped from the back of the bus as she sorted through what looked to be a lifetime's worth of clothing from enormous Louis Vuitton bags. "I mean, it's not like I could help being late. My driver got lost, but whatever."

When neither Mia nor Kylie responded, Lily kept chattering. "Maybe we could like switch off from week to week so that each of us would get to have the big room at some point," she suggested.

"Actually, Oklahoma was here first and she chose the front room so I took this one," Mia piped up as she entered the kitchenette. Kylie cringed as she listened to their conversation. It was already starting, the tense girl drama she'd so successfully avoided all throughout high school. *Passive aggressive insults and cold-shouldered silent treatments here we come*, she thought bitterly.

Thankfully the Vitamin Water people were smart enough to send along a mediator in the form of Brian Miller, a tech guy who was supposed to help the girls with the blog they had to keep up with during the tour. He wouldn't be with them for the whole tour, but he would meet up with them in a few cities to check in. *Probably to make sure we haven't murdered each other*.

Once they'd parked in Phoenix, Brian made his first appearance. "So each of you gets one of these," the freakishly tall but boyishly cute computer guy said as he handed each girl a tiny camera. "And you each have the app on your phone for the blog so you can upload pictures directly from there as well."

Kylie sat sandwiched between Lily and Mia in the booth in the media area of the bus. The zebra print upholstery was cute but she couldn't get comfortable. Lily was clearly holding some sort of grudge that Mia had gotten the master suite and her anger seemed to spill over onto Kylie as if she were somehow responsible.

But that was nothing compared to Mia. Tension radiated off of her in waves. It was so powerful it distracted Kylie while she tried to listen to Brian. With each passing minute, she was further convinced that she should've just stayed in Nashville and finished her album. *And hung out with Trace until he left on his tour*, her subconscious added. *Good plan. Just stay home and be the little woman. Go ahead and throw your career away before it even starts, just like Lauryn McCray*, it snapped at her.

"Kylie?" Brian was staring at her as if waiting for a response.

"I'm sorry, what was that?" She bit her lip and tried not to squirm under the awkwardness of the situation.

"I asked if you'd ever had a personal blog or website before." Brian smiled but she could hear Lily snickering beside her.

"Um, no. But I have been maintaining my own artist Facebook and Twitter accounts and stuff." Surely that counted for something.

"Okay, then. Mia, since Lily and Kylie are new to this, they're going to need your expertise. Think you can help them out?"

Kylie glanced over and watched Mia force a smile. "Sure, no problem," the girl next to her said. But it looked like the only thing Mia wanted to *help them out* of was the window.

CHAPTER Three

"You've got to be kidding me, Noel." Trace slammed his hand down as he pushed away from the table. "The answer is no. *Hell no.*"

Noel Davies crossed his arms and leaned back in his chair. "It wasn't a question, Corbin. Negotiations have ended. You got what you asked for. Dates are pretty much set. This is the deal. Take it or leave it."

Leave it, the voice inside his head commanded. But there was more to it than that. This was his chance to finally do a tour his way. Pick the venues, make the set list, play the songs he'd wanted to for so long. Stop being their damned puppet and focus on his kind of music. "And if I leave it?" he asked, being careful not to look at his manager or his agent as both would probably be getting good and pissed about now.

"Then you go it alone on your next album." Noel shrugged as if this was of no consequence to him whatsoever. *Cocky prick.*

Trace stood and paced for a minute. *Let the bastard sweat.* Pulling off his hat, he ran a hand through his hair before replacing it. Part of him wished he could talk to his girlfriend about now.

She was smart as hell and always had a clear-cut perspective when it came to music. Hell, she'd toured with his sorry ass when no one else would. And she was about to be huge. He could feel it. Whether or not he'd be by her side when she made it remained to be seen. But one thing was for sure—if he pansy-assed his way out of this deal then he definitely wouldn't be. At least not career-wise.

"And Gretchen is a sure thing? It's her or no one?" Feigning nonchalance, he leaned forward on the back of the chair he'd vacated.

"She is. You two are the best fit for this tour. She's already committed. If you pass, Bryce Parker has volunteered to replace you. Honestly, this was offered to you as a professional courtesy since you've been with the label the longest."

Trace glanced over at his manager to verify Noel's threat. Pauly Garrett nodded discreetly. *Damn.* Of course Parker would be happy to replace him. Dude was pretty much making a career of being his cheap knockoff stand-in as it was.

"I want my own bus," Trace demanded. Gretchen Gibson was even more of a mess than he was. He knew firsthand his girlfriend would lose her shit once she knew they were touring together, much less sharing a bus. Or she would just worry when she should be focusing on her own career. Either way he'd be causing her some type of stress. And that was the absolute last thing he wanted to do.

"You'll have yours. She'll just be on it as well. She doesn't have one of her own and right now the label isn't willing to spend any more money on either of you." Noel was starting to look bored with the whole thing.

Trace could feel his blood pressure going up. His mouth was dry with the need for a drink. It'd been over a week since he'd had one, and sobriety sucked so far. "So what you're saying is it's my tour but she's going to be on my bus whether I like it or not? Just to be clear."

Noel leaned forward, the sleeves of his suit jacket sliding up as he did. "Just to be clear, what I'm saying is what we have here are two major artists who let their personal problems interfere with business. In order to salvage not one but both of your careers, the label is going to give you each one more shot. One last shot, that is. It's going to be a medium to large venue tour with you and Gretchen as co-headliners. We're not going to spend any more money than we have already. Am I being clear enough for you, Mr. Corbin?"

His fists clenched. If Noel wasn't the son of the President of Capital Letter Records, he would punch the fucker in his smart mouth. As it was, his options were pretty limited. This was his dream tour. Even if it did involve the devil herself. He'd made his bed by skipping shows and acting like a jackass of epic proportions. Now he had to lie in it. Truth was, he knew exactly what his girlfriend would say. Damn near word for word. *There are people out there, real people with real problems, who show up to work day after day, night after night. But you think you can just do whatever the hell you feel like. Or not.* She also had a not-so-subtle way of reminding him how many people out there would gladly replace him. There was at least one tight jean-wearing fucker waiting in the wings that he knew of.

Rubbing his hands roughly over his face, he shoved up the sleeves of his plaid button-up and dropped back into his seat. "Where do I sign?"

Once he'd signed the next four months of his life away, he stood with his manager and prepared to leave. *Do not go get a drink,* he reminded himself.

"Hey, Trace—hold up a sec." Noel called out. "I need to speak with you for just a minute. Privately."

Trace turned as Pauly and his agent—a woman in her sixties named Maude who could easily have kicked all their asses—glared back at the suit.

"Relax, it's not about the tour." Noel smirked, and Trace nodded at his manager and agent as they let themselves out of the office.

He shut the door behind them and folded his arms. "What can I do for you, Davies? You've already fucked me up the ass. If you're expecting a blow job, I've got bad news for you."

"Cute. Actually I had a question for you. And I'd appreciate an honest answer."

Well, this was new. Noel Davies was usually more about giving orders than asking questions. Trace relaxed his stance and waited.

"It's about Kylie Ryans."

Swallowing hard, Trace scratched his jaw and stepped forward. "What about her?" If Noel Davies thought he was about to divulge his personal secrets like they were a couple of teenage girls at a sleepover, he was sorely mistaken.

"What do you think of her? About her?"

She's beautiful, smart, quick-witted as hell, and she possesses more raw talent than all of the artists at Capital Letter combined. Right now I'd much rather be buried deep inside of her, listening to her moan my name as she comes than standing here with your sorry ass.

What he actually said was, "She's all right. Why?"

Noel let out a snort as if he knew there was a lot more to it than that. *Tough shit, buddy.* "She's on our list of prospective artists to sign. The rumors alone about you and her have increased your album sales noticeably. I'd be interested in hearing your take on whether or not she'd be a good fit for this label."

Trace scoffed. "Oh, so *now* you want my input. Five minutes ago you were bending me over this table without the courtesy of lube, but now you need my advice?"

Noel shrugged. "Whether you think we should sign her or not isn't really that important to me. But if and when we do, we'd like to consider the possibility of you two touring together in the future. I wondered if you thought she was capable of holding her own in that situation—long term."

Been wondering that myself. "I think she can hold her own no matter who she tours with. I've never seen anyone as hungry for this as she is. And having seen her up on stage, I can tell you she's already more of a professional than I am. Not that that's necessarily saying much." Trace turned and pressed his hand against the door. *Aw hell.* The guy at least deserved some kind of a warning before dealing with his favorite hothead. He turned and smirked at the suit. "Do whatever you want. Just know she's not some pop princess pushover you can bully into becoming something she's not. Kylie Ryans would as soon tell you to fuck off as look at you." With that, he left.

CHAPTER Four

"Good night, Kansas City! Y'all are awesome! Thank you!" Kylie finished her set, struggling to catch her breath from the intense high performing always left her with. Mia stood in the wings and ignored her as she passed. So far there hadn't been much progress in that department.

Eleven weeks, she told herself. Surely she could make it through eleven weeks. Not that she really had a choice. She had rent to pay. And studio time didn't come cheap.

When she made her way back onto the bus, she thought for a second it had been vandalized. Clothes were everywhere, makeup was poured out all over the small table, and a false eyelash was stuck to the bathroom door. At least that was what it looked like. She started to back off the bus and yell for help when Lily came bounding out of her room.

"Oh thank God, you're back! I need help!"

She could say that again. Kylie stepped over a pair of red stilettos. "Yeah, um, what the hell happened in here?"

"Huh?" Lily glanced around then back at Kylie as if the bus did not, in fact, look like a hurricane had plowed straight through the center of it.

"Lily. Jesus. You have a room. This is ridic—"

"Kylie, there's no time for cleaning up! Mia's onstage now and I still haven't picked out what I'm wearing! And I need help getting these damn eyelashes on. Why Vitamin Water couldn't spring for some hair and makeup people is beyond me." The girl took a breath long enough to look around.

Kylie noticed that one eyelash did look significantly thinner than the other. Snatching the other one off the bathroom door, she handed it over.

Lily's face lit up as if she'd been handed the keys to Disneyland. "Ah! Thank you! I've been looking everywhere for that!" Kylie couldn't help but smile. The girl was pretty easy to please. She and Mia had soothed her hurt about the big room by offering to let her close the next few shows.

"You're welcome. But, Lily, seriously. This—"

"Okay, look—here's the red dress, and I'd wear the red stilettos with it. Or should I wear the cream dress with the jean jacket and boots?" Before Kylie had time to answer, Lily grabbed another outfit that had been lying on the counter by the coffeemaker. "Ooh! Or maybe the silver sleeveless one with my pink heels. Or black boots."

A dull, throbbing sensation began to make its way to Kylie's temples. "Um, I like the red dress. Maybe wear the jean jacket and boots with it? Or the red heels. Whichever." She watched as Lily chewed her lip, and a dimple appeared in her left cheek. The sixteen-year-old suddenly seemed very sixteen.

"You're a genius!" Lily leapt at her, wrapping her in a hug she was both unprepared for and unable to return before the girl grabbed an armful of clothing and darted into her room.

After shaking off the overly affectionate encounter and carefully sidestepping the landmines of Lily's crap, including an enormous hair dryer with something on the end of it that looked like it could inflict some serious pain, she made her way to her room. She'd no sooner stepped inside her haven, where she was safe from Lily Taite, than the girl yelled out again. "Kylie! I still need your help with this eyelash! I can't get—Ow! Oh God, ow! Please come help me!"

Sighing, she headed back towards Lily's room. Touring with Trace was starting to look like Heaven compared to this.

Once she'd removed the spiky eyelash from Lily's eyeball and glued it in place where it should be, she told the girl to have a great show and finally escaped to her room. She wasn't a neat freak by any means, but her version of messy was carefully contained chaos, whereas Lily's version was more holy-fuck-we've-been-robbed.

After she'd changed out of the black dress she'd performed in, she slipped into her jammies. Grabbing the cellphone from the charger on her nightstand, she collapsed onto her bed.

She was just about to text Trace and see if he was up for a Skype date when she saw she already had several texts from Cora reminding her to blog, Tweet, and post a Facebook message about the show. And she was supposed to post photos as well. *Damn. Why can't I just freaking sing?*

Well, she hadn't taken any pictures inside The Hangout, the music cafe where she'd just performed, so she made her way to the main area of the bus and snapped a picture of the damage Lily had caused. She posted it online with the caption: **Girls are slobs. Note to self: Do not ever leave Lily Taite alone on the bus again.**

She Tweeted about how awesome Kansas City was and how excited she was about next week's shows in Colorado and Texas. She commented on a few photos that fans had posted of them together before tonight's show. Finally, after she'd hopefully done enough to please Cora, she sat back down on her bed and texted Trace.

Hey babe. Just finished my set. Lily Taite reminds me of Rae. If Rae was on crack. Miss you...

She knew he was busy with planning his upcoming tour, so she didn't expect a response right away. But it came a minute later.

Miss you too. That sounds terrifying.

She laughed out loud and sent him the photo she'd taken of the bus. Within a few seconds he responded.

What the hell happened???

She explained about Hurricane Lily. And how she didn't realize how good she had it touring with him. He sent a winky face. His response time began to increase. When she heard Mia come back on the bus, she knew she needed to get to the computer before the other girl did. One computer and three girls was a shitty idea to begin with. As was sharing a bathroom with Lily. She was kind of starting to wish she'd taken the suite after all.

Skype date? She texted as fast as her fingers would allow. Several minutes passed and no message came.

Her bedroom door slid open and a red-faced Mia Montgomery glared at her. "Did you tell Lily she could wear my jacket and my boots?"

Kylie set her phone down on the nightstand. "Um, no I didn't."

Mia folded her arms over the tight blue T-shirt she was wearing. "I just passed her as she was heading to the stage. She was wearing my shit. I asked her what the hell she was thinking and she said you told her to wear that."

Her accusatory tone had Kylie's hackles rising. "Okay, first of all, I came onto this disaster of a bus and was accosted by the blonde fairy of destruction herself. She threw a bunch of outfits at me—ones she'd already picked out—and I made a suggestion." She didn't mention the surgical procedure she'd performed on Lily's eye.

Mia huffed out a loud breath. "She really is a fucking slob."

At that, Kylie grinned. "I Tweeted about it. Put a picture on the blog, too."

"No you didn't."

"I did." She shrugged even though she was beginning to wonder if what she'd posted would hurt the girl's feelings. Lily was a spoiled pain in the ass but she meant well and didn't deserve to be made fun of, online or otherwise. She wasn't out and out hostile like Mia at least.

"Maybe I should post something about people not touching my stuff without permission." Mia snorted. "Anyways, I'm going to go grab some food and a few drinks with a couple of roadies. Later."

Part of Kylie wanted to ask her to wait. To stay and chat or maybe just tell her what the hell her problem was. But she knew that might not be the best idea. And Mia seemed to be in a hurry to get away from her. She didn't miss that she very clearly wasn't invited to dinner.

Once the girl was gone, she glanced at her phone.

I'm on Skype. Where u at, Kylie Lou?

His text was from a few minutes ago. She hadn't even realized she'd been chatting with Mia that long.

She bolted to the media area and flipped the computer open. Crap, it was off. She hit the button to turn it on and waited. And waited. His schedule was packed in the mad rush to get his *No Apologies* tour going. If she missed him tonight, there was no telling when she'd get to see his handsome face again. Finally the computer screen came to life and she typed in her username and password. She clicked on the Skype icon. While it logged her in, she tapped out a quick text.

Sorry, was talking to Mia. Getting on Skype now.

When her chat window opened up, he was marked as offline. Damn. She glanced down at her phone but he hadn't responded. She propped her elbows on the table and rubbed her eyes. It shouldn't be that big of a deal. So she'd missed him. But it was a big deal. As much as she hated herself for it, it was suddenly hard to swallow. Because she missed him.

CHAPTER Five

"Have I mentioned what a bad idea I think this is?" Pauly Garrett asked as he scratched his goatee.

"You have. Several times. Now let's go." Trace opened the truck door and got out. He walked into the Tin Roof with his manager and glanced around for her. He wasn't all that thrilled about her choice of meeting place or the fact that they were about to be going on a sixteen-week tour together. But this was what the label had decided, and he was going to man up and deal.

She was in a back booth. Several shots were lined up on the table in front of her. He and his manager made their way over.

"Gretchen." He tipped his hat in her direction and sat down in the seat across from her. Pauly pulled up a chair to the end of the table and nodded.

"Trace." She nodded back, her jet black hair sweeping over one eye as she did. "I see you brought your keeper along."

He raised an eyebrow at her but didn't bite. If she was trying to get a rise out of him, she was going to be disappointed. He wasn't that guy anymore. At least, he was trying not to be. "Gretchen, you remember Pauly, my manager."

"Not really." She shrugged and downed her first shot. Tequila. He could smell it. Same old Gretchen. "I bet he remembers me though." She wiped her mouth with the back of her hand.

"How could I forget," the man answered dryly.

"I'm pretty unforgettable." She winked at Trace. *So much for letting bygones be bygones.*

"So what's the deal, Gretch? You gonna be able to get through this tour without passing out or falling off stage? 'Cause I gotta say, I'm pretty damned sure the label is setting us up to fail. Killing two fuck-ups with one stone and all that." He propped his elbows on the table and waited for her to either promise she was getting her shit together or tell him to screw right off. With Gretchen Gibson, he never knew what to expect.

"Aw, is wittle Twace worried about me?" She snorted and took another shot. "Relax. I'm a big girl. I can handle myself." She shoved a shot in his direction and half of it spilled onto the table. "Let's toast. To not having to apologize for being who we are."

"I'm good." He slid the shot aside, away from both of them. "And yeah, I hear you're handling yourself real well these days. Your crazy shit makes mine look normal. At least when I get plastered I have the decency not to show up for my shows. You, on the other hand, find it entertaining to pass out, vomit, and piss yourself on stage." He leaned closer to her, moving the last remaining shot even farther out of her reach. "I've been where you are, Gretchen. Recently. And I'm not going back there. I'm also not going to let you screw up my chance to show everyone that I still want this. That I deserve it."

Dark, heavily lined eyes raked over him cold and hard. "What are you trying to say, Corbin? That I *don't* deserve it?" Her voice was always kind of throaty and rough. It was what made her songs so sexy and unique. Like her. But he saw more than that now. More than the edgy dangerous badass vibe she was trying to put off. He saw the pain. The desperation. He saw it because he was finally learning to recognize it in himself.

He shook his head, remembering how cornered he'd felt when people started telling him he had a problem. "No. That's not what

I'm saying at all." He took a deep breath and tried to explain better. "Look, I'm done with drinking my pain away. And yeah, it's hard, and I'm not exactly in complete control of it. But Pauly has a friend. His name is Camden Reynolds. Dr. Camden Reynolds."

Gretchen smirked. "Oh, good. Pauly finally came out of the closet then." She turned to Pauly and grinned. "And you landed yourself a doctor. Congratulations."

Trace watched as his manager grimaced. He hated Gretchen. Most people did. But Trace couldn't bring himself to. He saw too much of himself in her. Not that he necessarily liked himself much. But he was working on that. "He's an addiction specialist. He can go on the tour with us and you can talk to him any time you feel like things are getting out of control."

Gretchen's steely gray eyes darkened. "No."

Trace cleared his throat. He'd known this wouldn't be easy. He'd tried being nice, but women like Gretchen didn't really respond to that. Nice guys were the ones they crushed to dust under their boot heels and stepped over to get to some sorry son of a bitch who'd treat them like shit. He knew—he'd been a sorry son of a bitch most of his life. "Okay, let me rephrase. See, I wasn't asking you. I was telling you. Dr. Reynolds is basically going to be at my beck and call. If you start fucking things up on the tour, he will intervene. And so will I." He leaned back in anticipation of the anger that was about to come spewing out onto him.

Surprisingly, Gretchen just glared back at him. When neither of them said anything, Pauly spoke up. "Look, both of you are in poor standing with the label. They think you're both drunks who can't handle your careers and aren't worth their time or money. Either this tour can be your way of showing them you're still the kind of artists they want to support or you can prove them right." He shrugged as if he were okay with whichever option they chose.

Trace nodded in agreement and turned his focus back to Gretchen. "What do you say, Gretch? Can we show those suit-wearing bastards that we can do this? Or should we call it a day and cancel the tour?"

She reached forward, grabbing the shot in front of Pauly

and downing it before anyone could blink. Standing abruptly, she stumbled but regained control of herself before Trace or his manager could offer to help her. She stopped next to where Trace sat and leaned down to his level. He could smell the tequila on her breath. Thankfully he'd never been much of a fan. If she'd been drinking bourbon, his mouth probably would've watered at the scent. "Hm. What do I say?" He turned to look at her, his stomach clenching at the redness in her eyes. The vacant stare on her face. She looked like hammered hell. That was what Kylie Lou must've seen when she looked at him. How or why she'd thought him worthy of her was beyond him. Gretchen let out a little snort and continued on with her response. "I say it's a shame. You used to be *a lot* more fun." With that, she sauntered away from them, over to the bar where she propped up on a stool and began flirting with the bartender.

"Well…that answers that," Pauly said.

Trace dropped his head into his hands. "Well…fuck."

CHAPTER Six

"Where in the hell is my left boot, Lily? I'm serious!" Mia shouted from the back of the bus where she was digging through her closet.

"I don't know! Hey, have you seen my straightener?" Lily called back. "Oh, is this your boot?"

Kylie stepped out of her room and ducked just in time to narrowly miss being nailed in the head by a flying Frye boot. They'd just parked outside the Fall Festival fairgrounds in Denver where the girls would be performing in a few hours. She picked up the boot that had nearly maimed her and carried it into Mia's room. "Looking for this?"

Mia looked up from the pile of clothes she was digging through. Relief smoothed her features as she crossed the room and took the boot. "Yup."

You're welcome. Two weeks together and Mia was still an ice queen set on freezing Kylie out. She'd even started being friendlier to Lily. But every time Kylie walked into a room, Mia's posture stiffened and her eyes went hard. *Like I ran over her favorite dog. And laughed about it.*

The Pistol Annies were blaring from Mia's iPod. "They're my favorite," Kylie told her, nodding at the dock.

Mia raised her eyebrows as if to ask why the hell she thought she gave a damn. Then she stepped over to the vanity and began rifling through her makeup as if Kylie weren't even there.

"Hey, can we talk for a sec?" When Mia ignored her, she tried again. Louder this time. "Mia! Can you turn that down for just a minute? Please?"

Mia glanced over at her. "What?"

Kylie sighed and made a series of hand motions as if she knew sign language or baseball signals. Mia gave her a weird look and silenced the iPod. "What the hell?"

Kylie leaned her head out of the room. "Lil, can you come in Mia's room, please?"

Mia glared as if she thought Kylie was staging an intervention. Kylie forced a small smile. It wasn't anything like that. The only person who needed an intervention was Lily the clothes whore, but that wasn't what she wanted to talk about either.

Once Lily stepped inside the room, Kylie backed up so she could look at both of them while she spoke. "Um, I wanted to talk to you both. About how we close the show each night."

"Oh no, Oklahoma. You are not going to strong-arm us into letting you close every night. I don't give a shit who your boyfriend is." Mia crossed her arms over her chest and took a step closer to Lily.

Whoa. What the hell? Kylie backed up a step, nearly backing into Mia's dresser. "Wow. Thanks, Mia. You can cross being a bitch to me off your list for today. For the record, I would never do something like that. And technically we've closed the last few shows together—singing that song the Vitamin Water people told us to. And that's what I wanted to talk about."

"What about it?" Lily asked, plopping on the bed.

"Do you know who wrote it?" Kylie asked. She knew because Chaz had told her.

"No, why?" Lily glanced over at her reflection in Mia's mirror. Girl had some serious attention deficit issues.

"Lauryn McCray wrote it," Mia offered. "So what?"

Kylie bit her lip. If it didn't bother Mia, maybe it shouldn't bother her. Except…it did. A lot. "It's kind of strange, don't you think? She wrote it when she thought she was going to be on this tour. Now she's not and we're still singing her song." In the past week, the rumors had been confirmed. Lauryn was, in fact, pregnant. By her agent, Scotty Brasher, who no one knew much about except that he wasn't commenting publicly about Lauryn or the baby.

What made Kylie even more uncomfortable was the fact that the song was called *All My Life* and was about working hard to realize your dreams. Every time she sang the line *I gave it all up, gave it all away, dreamin' of the day when it would be worth it, knowin' I deserved it,* she felt sick. Like her heart was plummeting to her gut. Lauryn had worked hard and had overcome a pretty rough past, according to her CMT Backstory, to get where she was. Then she got pregnant and her career was pretty much over. Or on hold indefinitely at least. And now Kylie, Mia, and Lily sang her song every night. It was weird. And depressing.

"I don't get it," Lily said, pulling her hair into a high ponytail and glancing back in the mirror as she did so.

"Suddenly Oklahoma here has a conscience." Mia snorted. "Boo hoo. Lauryn got knocked up. Not our fault, and I bet she made enough money selling that song to decorate one hell of a baby nursery. So I don't see what the big deal is."

Kylie frowned. Why the hell did Mia think she didn't have a conscience before? Whatever. That wasn't the point. "The big deal is, that could be any of us. And if something happened and I couldn't be on the tour, I don't know how I'd feel about three random chicks singing my song—you know?"

"Couldn't be me. I'm a virgin," Lily announced.

Mia rolled her eyes. "Good for you." She looked at Kylie for a few seconds before adding, "Okay. So what song are the three of us going to sing if we scrap that one? If we're even allowed to do that?"

She hadn't gotten that far yet. "I don't know."

"Ooh, we could write something together," Lily suggested, practically bouncing up and down with excitement.

Well, that was one idea.

"We have a show in a few hours. We'd have to write fast." Mia's voice was even but Kylie could see she was interested. And that she was only looking at Lily. She was going to try and shove Kylie out of this too. *Like hell she is.*

Kylie stepped forward so they couldn't ignore her. "Anybody got a pen?"

Three hours, two dozen sheets of paper, and more dirty looks from Mia than Kylie could count later, they had a song. Or something that looked like a song at least. They'd get to practice a few times at sound check and then give it a go for real. Misty Cole, their contact at Vitamin Water, had been surprised about their request but said she didn't see any problem with them performing a new song instead of Lauryn's. Kylie was relieved. Every time they sang it, she'd pictured herself having to tell Trace she was pregnant. How he would react and how much it would hurt both of their careers. Before she saw him again, she was going to buy the biggest box of condoms she could find. And she was going to start taking her birth control pills religiously.

"Think the audience will like it?" Lily asked after they'd finished rehearsing.

"Hope so," Kylie answered. Mia said nothing. She was in one of her moods where she acted like they were beneath her. Kylie knew twenty-one-year-old Mia felt like Lily was too young to be touring. She'd said so out loud. And Kylie kind of agreed. But what the hell her problem was with her was a mystery. Unless…it was the one thing they didn't discuss. He who shall not be named. She really hoped that wasn't what was bothering Mia. Because it was sure as hell starting to bother her.

It was Mia's turn to close the show. Once she'd finished her set, Kylie and Lily joined her on stage. Kylie's heart was racing as she took her seat on the stool between the two of them. They were going acoustic style for the debut of the song they'd written together. *Your Time to Shine* reminded Kylie so much of Trace she feared she'd tear up during her solo. But she sucked it up and sang the first verse. *Don't know who deals the cards that decide the hand we're dealt. But I know I've seen my lows and I see you goin' down that road.* The other two joined her on the bridge. *And it's a long, dark path. No end in sight. Just before you give up, you'll see the light. 'Cause, baby, it's your time to shine.*

Lily's clear voice was soft as she sang her solo. *You made your bed on a wish and a prayer. Looking up on that stage sayin' one day you'd be there. But it was a long, dark path. No end in sight. Just before you gave up, you saw the light. Baby, it's your time to shine.* The three of them harmonized as they sang the part Lily was so adamant about adding. *Ooohh oooh ooohhooo. Ooohh ooh ooohhoo. Baby, it's your time to shine.*

Mia's voice was strong and had a deep southern twang similar to Kylie's, even though Kylie knew she was actually from Detroit. But to hear her sing, anyone would think she was from the Deep South. *And that spotlight's bright when you finally get there. Not much you can count on, besides a dream and a prayer. And they're all gonna say that you'll fall any day. But lucky for you, you know that's not true. They just wanna be in your shoes.*

Kylie sucked in a breath to sing her final solo. *When you fall back down, on that unforgivin' ground, that's okay. 'Cause if there's one thing you've learned along the way, it's how to pick yourself back up. You didn't get here on luck.*

The three of them sang the final chorus and another string of Lily's Oooh oooh oohoos. When the song ended, Kylie took a deep breath. Her ears were filled with applause. *Thank God.* She smiled and glanced over at Mia and Lily. They'd written and sang together now, and even if they didn't like each other very much, she respected the hell out of both of them.

CHAPTER Seven

"*How's* that pretty little girlfriend of yours?" Rose asked Trace as she touched up his makeup. He couldn't help but grin. He'd just seen Kylie's latest post on her tour blog. There was video link of her and the two girls she was on tour with singing a song they'd written together. He'd been so damn proud watching her he'd nearly burst. They didn't get to talk much with their busy schedules, but he checked in with her blog every day, hoping for a picture of her beautiful face. God, he missed that face.

"Too good for me, Rose. Too good for me."

The woman guffawed and slapped him lightly on the shoulder. "Nah, you're not so bad."

Trace gave her his best wounded puppy expression. "Then how come you never would give me the time of day?" He winked at the woman, who was well into her fifties, maybe older. Though she dyed her hair and wore enough makeup that, from a distance, you wouldn't guess she was a day over thirty or so.

"Now, darlin', you know I'd be happy to use you for your body, but I'm a happily married woman." She shrugged.

Trace laughed out loud. Rose always was good for a laugh.

"My loss, sweetheart." He jumped out of the chair, momentarily distracted by the teasing. Today he and Gretchen had their promotional photo shoot for the tour. They'd be in a bar, play-acting like they were drinking and throwing punches. Except Gretchen would probably actually be drinking and he might actually punch someone before the day was over.

He sauntered into Whiskey Jacks like it wasn't the absolute last place he wanted to be. Even though it was. The label had rented the private room out for the day so it was empty save for himself, Pauly, a photographer, and a bunch of assistants. Most of who were probably useless.

"Okay, let's get some lights over by the pool table. We'll do a few shots there." A man dressed in black with a nasally voice that was already grating on his nerves was giving orders. "And somebody line some shots up on the bar. And grab a few bottles and set them in the background."

Trace took advantage of the rare moment of free time to text Kylie good morning and that he'd seen her video and loved the song. Before he had a chance to see if she'd texted back, Nasally Voice Dude turned to him. "Okay, Mr. Corbin, let's get a few of you alone while we wait for Gretchen."

Great. Day one of this shit and they were already "waiting" for Gretchen. Professionalism was not her strong suit. Not that he was necessarily one to talk.

"Sure thing." Trace stepped over to the spot by the pool table where the photographer indicated. Someone handed him a pool stick, and for a moment he just wanted to be a regular guy. Shooting some pool on a Friday night with the guys after a long week of busting his hump wherever he worked. He could practically see Kylie sauntering over and challenging him to a game of pool. She'd probably kick his ass at that too. His girl was full of surprises.

"Mr. Corbin, can you lean down and pretend to line up a shot?"

Trace glanced down at the table. "Uh, I could, but there's no cue ball." He stepped around and checked each pocket, but the cue ball was nowhere to be seen.

"Okay, forget the cue ball. Just lean down and pose like you're about to sink the orange ball."

"Yeah, I would. But I'd look like a jackass aiming my stick at the nine ball when there's no cue ball on the table. Isn't the idea for it to look like Gretchen and I are out on the town actually playing pool? You can't play pool without a cue ball."

The photographer lowered his camera and rubbed his temples.

Trace huffed out a breath. "Dude, I'm not trying to be a dick here. I can stand with the stick and look like I'm planning my next shot or whatever, but I'm not going to pose like I'm a fucking moron who doesn't realize he needs a cue ball to play pool." Trace lifted the stick behind his head and rested his arms on it while he waited for someone to use their brain and realize how asinine the whole thing was.

"Can somebody please get Mr. Corbin a cue ball? Now!" an assistant called out and a few people scrambled to do as they were told. The photographer glared at him. Trace glanced at Pauly and shrugged. His manager just shook his head.

This was the part he hated. He didn't want to "pretend" to shoot pool. He really didn't want to be in a bar period. And he sure as hell didn't want to be arguing with some tight-ass photographer about the importance of a cue ball. He wanted to be at home, snuggled up on the couch with his gorgeous girlfriend. Writing music, watching a movie, making love. Any and all of those options would be better than this.

"We have a cue ball," someone called out. The cue ball in question was passed to several people before it made its way to the table. Once it was in place, Trace leaned down and pretended to shoot. He held that pose until his back ached. He'd unloaded several hundred bales of straw at the farm last week. When he couldn't take any more, he stood. He met the photographer's gaze and the expression he found there said he was still supposed to be bent over the table like his bitch. Oh well.

"Now what?" He turned and cracked his back.

Before the photographer could answer him, there was a commotion up near the bar. "Actually, Ms. Gibson, those are just for looks," an assistant told Gretchen as she waltzed in and snatched a shot off the bar. Her sunglasses were still on and Trace had a feeling he knew why.

"Where the hell is the fun in that?" she asked as she downed the shot and set the empty glass back down on the bar. The assistant grabbed it and refilled it.

"Nice of you to show," Trace called out to her.

"You're welcome." She finally took off her glasses as Rose converged on her with a handful of brushes. The woman wore a tool belt full of makeup for God's sakes. The world was a weird place.

But one look at Gretchen and he was grateful for the woman's emergency makeup skills. Gretchen was hungover as hell. Normally she was kind of pretty, but today her face looked like road kill. Her eyes were bloodshot and puffy, the skin beneath managing to be swollen and saggy at the same time. He knew she was a few years older than him but that was still too young to have deep-set lines around her mouth. Without makeup she looked like she was pushing fifty. She made Rose look like Miss America.

"Rough night, Gretch?" he asked quietly as he approached.

"Wouldn't you like to know?" She sneered at him from under Rose's meticulous hands.

Okay then. Operation Make Peace with Gretchen was a no-go. Abort. "Well, is it okay with you if we go ahead and get this shit over with then?"

"Yep, I'm ready." She hopped down off the stool even though Rose was still attempting to swipe brushes all over her face. "Cut it out. That's what Photoshop is for, dammit," Gretchen snapped, leaning away from the makeup woman's efforts.

"Easy, cowgirl. Don't be a bitch to Rose. She's trying to help you. God love her, I'm not even sure that's possible."

"Fuck off, Corbin. Really not in the mood for your shit today."

He laughed harshly. "My shit? I'm not the one who was—"

"Okay, everybody smile," the photographer interrupted. On cue, Trace and Gretchen turned and smiled wildly. *I am a fucking puppet of epic proportions*, he thought to himself. *Just what I always wanted to be when I grew up.*

He kicked his pride along as he posed with Gretchen at the bar and at the pool table. The photographer had him blatantly check out Gretchen's ass while she bent over and pretended to take a shot. Then he had one of the assistants step in and stare at her ass as well. They did a little scene where Trace caught the guy staring and he got to throw a few pretend punches at the dude. Sadly, that was the highlight of his day.

The photographer got pissy when Trace demanded his shot glasses be filled with water instead of alcohol during the part of the session where he and Gretchen were ordered to pose like they were taking body shots off each other. *This is not going to go over well. Sorry, Kylie Lou.* He'd have to be sure and tell her Gretchen was hungover, had breath from hell, and smelled like a homeless guy.

If he ever got time to talk to her that was.

CHAPTER Eight

"Kyyliieee Ryans, is that you?" a female voice shouted over the noise on the street. The girls had just finished their sound check in Oklahoma City. She looked up and saw Lulu crossing the street and heading towards the bus. Kylie squealed, actually squealed, and ran to her friend like they were a couple in a Hollywood movie.

"Lulu! Damn, I didn't realize how much I was missin' you, girl!" Actually, she did. It felt so good to see a smiling face she could have cried.

The girls hugged and then her friend pulled back. "Yeah? Those wenches giving you hell? Need me to cunt punch one of them? Or both of them?"

She laughed, even though the tension on the bus had gotten so bad she was probably one more dirty look or rude comment away from a nervous breakdown. "I can handle it. But it's really good to see your face! Speaking of faces, where's Carmen?"

Lulu grimaced. "She's with her new fella." She shrugged and shifted the enormous knock-off designer bag she carried to her other shoulder. "Remember Harley Hudson? Worked at the gas station in town?"

Kylie racked her brain but came up with nothing. "Um, no."

"Yeah, no reason why you should. Anyways, him and his dad opened a body repair shop and hired Carmen as a receptionist. Pretty soon Carmen was doing more than answering phones and filing receipts. If you know what I mean." Lulu waggled her eyebrows.

"Ah."

"Yeah, well. They're a thing now. He's all right, I guess." Suddenly her friend's eyes lit up and she smiled. "Oh! Actually he has a house between here and Pride. Supposed to be having some big party tonight to celebrate the success of the new business. You wanna go?"

"Good God, yes. I *need* to go. If I don't get off that bus I might go in-fucking-sane. Three girls were never meant to live like that. It was so much easier with Trace."

Lulu snorted. "Yeah, I bet it was." She let out a dramatic sigh. "Guess all my bitches got dudes now."

Kylie slapped her friend lightly on the arm. "Hey, I'm no one's bitch."

Lulu giggled. "Uh, I think you might be Trace Corbin's bitch. Maybe a little?"

She bit her lip to contain the grin his name brought to her face. "Nah. He's my bitch."

"Hey, speaking of bitches, want to take a drive to Pride and go roll Darla's new house?"

She struggled to make sense of what her friend had just said. "What do you mean, her *new* house?"

Lulu's panic-stricken expression made her stomach tighten. "Um, I'm sorry, Ky. I thought you knew. She sold your old house and bought one on the nicer side of town."

So that was what she'd done with the money Trace had paid her to keep quiet then. Rage flooded her and she struggled to breathe normally as not to alarm her friend. "I can't believe she sold my daddy's house. No, wait, I can believe it. She never gave a shit about him." She fought off a sob as tears threatened to fill her eyes. Her daddy had deserved better than what he'd gotten. He'd deserved to be loved.

"Don't worry. I'll pay the high school football team to roll her house every weekend if you want. Not like there's anything better to do in Pride."

Kylie contemplated that offer as they walked to the bus. "If you run out of money, let me know. I'll donate to the cause."

"Eh, I can always flash ' a boob or two if the funding runs out."

Kylie laughed. "So who bought my house?"

Lulu tilted her head to the side and was quiet for a brief moment. "You know, I'm not sure actually. One day it was for sale and the next it was sold. But no one's moved in yet. Maybe when you're rich and famous you can buy it back from them. If you want."

"Right, 'cause fame and fortune are just around the corner." Kylie rolled her eyes and began giving Lulu a tour of the bus. Well, the best tour she could give as they tripped and stumbled over all of Lily's crap. The most upsetting thing about the hellacious mess was that she was actually starting to get used to it.

After the show, Kylie introduced Mia and Lily to Lulu, who kept insisting she was going by Olivia now. Not that Kylie ever intended to actually call her that.

"So that song y'all sang at the end was pretty awesome," her best friend said.

Mia and Lily mumbled, "Thanks," almost in unison. And then the four girls sat in awkward silence. Until Kylie couldn't take it anymore.

"So, um, Lu and I are going to a party but I'll be back later."

"Ohh, I wanna go," Lily squealed.

Damn. The most exciting thing about going out was getting the hell away from them. Actually, she was kind of used to Lily. But five more minutes in close quarters with Mia was going to result in bloodshed. Or some serious bitch-slapping. Kylie could take it if she had to, but Lulu wasn't one to keep her hands to herself.

"Oh-kay," Kylie said slowly. "Um, Mia? You comin'?"

Mia smirked and made a big show of rolling her eyes. "Much as I love a good old-fashioned hillbilly hoedown, I'm going to have to pass."

Thank you, Jesus.

"I'll be sure and French kiss my cousin for you," Lulu piped up. *Oh hell.*

Mia's eyebrows rose nearly to her hairline.

"We should get going." Kylie linked her arm with Lulu's and all but dragged her off the bus as Lily bounded out behind them. "Later," she called out to Mia, knowing she wouldn't get an answer.

Lulu still had lots to say though. "What the fuck is her problem? Batteries go dead in her vibrator?"

Kylie snorted. "Not in front of the kids," she said, jerking her head back towards Lily.

"Hey!" Lily whined.

Her friend stopped walking and turned to face her. "Kylie, I'm serious. That's bullshit. You shouldn't have to put up with that." She watched as the girl she loved like a sister shook her head. "You need to confront that uptight fucktwat like *yesterday*. Find out what the hell her deal is."

Kylie said nothing as the three of them climbed into Lulu's car. She had a feeling she knew *exactly* what Mia's problem was. What she didn't know was whether or not she actually wanted to hear about it.

CHAPTER Nine

Trace paced back and forth along the glass wall of the conference room. It was day three of negotiations with Gretchen, her "people," and the label. So far most of the tour was scheduled, but due to her past transgressions, Gretchen was currently banned from a few of the establishments that had originally been on the itinerary.

Kylie had texted him twice asking if he had a minute to talk. He texted her back that he was in a meeting and would call her soon. That was two hours ago. She said she was going to a party with some friends near her hometown so he figured she was fine. He just wished he'd been able to call and make sure everything was okay. Screw it.

"Look, I don't see what the hell I'm doing here. I'm not banned from anywhere so just schedule whatever places will let Gretchen in." He smirked. "If you can find enough of them."

"Go to hell, Corbin," she snapped at him.

"Pretty sure I'm already there, sweetheart." He pulled his phone out and caught Pauly's eye. He jerked his head towards the door but his manager shook his head no. Christ. He was a grown man for fuck's sakes. A grown man with a beautiful girl waiting for his phone call. Not to mention the fact that he felt like if he didn't hear her sweet, soothing voice soon he was going to knock someone's teeth out. He hadn't had sex or a drink in weeks and the throbbing in his head was constant.

"Noel, pardon me, but I'm dealing with a family situation. You mind if I step out to make a call?"

Noel Davies glared at him but didn't say anything. That was good enough for him. Trace stepped out into the waiting area outside the conference room. He hadn't even meant to say a "family situation." He'd planned to say he was dealing with a situation. No description necessary. But in a way, Kylie was a part of his family. She was the first person who stood up to him. The first one who cared enough to risk everything and face him down.

He pulled up her number on his phone, grinning at the picture of her he'd taken just after they'd made love for the last time before she left to go on tour. It was a close-up of her face, and her clear blue eyes had that sexy sleepy look he loved so much. It rang several times and then a burst of noise came through the line.

"Kylie Lou, you there?"

"Trace," she said, sounding relieved to hear from him. Her voice was so sweet it warmed him from the inside out, but it was edged with a bit of panic too.

"Hey, baby. Sorry I couldn't call sooner. Everything okay?"

The noise in the background that sounded like music began to fade. But other voices took its place. "Yeah....sorry...party in the middle...where."

"I'm losin' you, darlin'. Can you hear me?" He hated not knowing if she was okay. Maybe he'd take a drive to Oklahoma tonight. Tomorrow's seven a.m. rehearsal be damned.

"Yeah. I'm here. Can you hear me okay?"

"I can now. You havin' a good time? Behavin' yourself?" He was thankful she was the kind of girl who always behaved herself. Except when she was around him.

"Yeah, um, Lily had too much to drink and she's sick...me and Lulu...her in the house."

"I'm losin' you again. Sounds like you're dealing with a

situation of your own though. Guess I need to get back in this meeting with Gretchen's people." Oh shit. He hadn't even told her about Gretchen yet. Panic swept over him as he realized this was probably not the ideal time to discuss it.

"Gretchen who?" Kylie asked evenly, suddenly sounding eerily calm. Great. *Now* he had her full attention and perfect reception.

"Uh, yeah. Did I forget to mention that Gretchen Gibson is co-headlining with me on the tour?"

"I don't know. *Did* you forget to mention that? Or…just…not…to tell me?" The connection began to break up again. She didn't sound mad exactly. Just a little hurt maybe. Which was worse. He'd hurt her enough when they were on tour together. He'd sincerely hoped he'd never hurt her again. Looked like that was probably out of the question.

He didn't want to have to explain this with their connection like it was. "No, I mean, no I didn't not want to tell you. Shit. That didn't make sense." He ran a hand through his hair and glanced around. A receptionist and a few people sat in the waiting area. He would much rather have this particular conversation somewhere more private. Preferably in person. "Listen, it wasn't my choice. The label forced her on me and I was trying to do what you said. Suck it up and work like everyone else has to, you know?"

"Oh hell. Lily just got sick again. How about I call you later or tomorrow and you can tell me how you ended up on tour with the female version of yourself?"

"Ouch, Kylie Lou. Words can hurt, you know."

She laughed and he couldn't have kept the smile off his face if he'd wanted to. Her laugh was almost as beautiful as she was.

After they hung up, he returned to the conference room. Or his own personal hell. Whichever.

After another long, stressful hour of nailing down the exact tour schedule, Trace went back to his place, a penthouse apartment downtown. Every part of him ached to go grab a drink. Or six. These past few weeks had been hell and he was desperate for some type of distraction. He held off, but just barely.

Finishing off the last of the pizza he'd had delivered the night before, he half-watched SportsCenter while keeping an eye on his phone. He'd never expected to miss that girl so much. He'd never been the kind of guy to miss anyone.

He hated not having her close enough to touch. To talk to. He needed that sweet, sassy mouth to kiss. The three bottles of Shiner Bock in his fridge called out to him. *It's just a few beers.* It wasn't enough to get drunk. Hopefully it'd ease the sting of missing his girl. The bottles clinked together as he pulled one from the fridge, making a comforting sound he was familiar with.

As he scrolled through the previous messages Kylie had sent, phone in one hand, cold bottle in the other, he nearly laughed at himself. He was pretty sure reading old text messages just to feel close to her was a pretty sad-ass move. But damn, what he wouldn't give to have her here. To be able to take her to bed every night and wake up to that beautiful face every morning. *Slow your roll, Corbin.* She was nineteen years old for fuck's sake. At nineteen he didn't know whether he was coming or going most days, much less how he was going to spend the rest of his life. Yeah, he had plans for a future with Kylie, but he was going to make certain she got to experience whatever she wanted before she hitched her wagon to his sorry ass for life. If she even wanted to, that was.

The beer was cold, soothing like he knew it would be. He finished off the third and tossed the bottles in the trash. There. He was straight. He wasn't itching to run to the liquor store.

When she hadn't texted or called by midnight, he started getting ready for bed— figuring she was busy with her drunk friend. He'd been there. Well, he'd usually *been* the drunk friend. But he understood.

Just before he crashed out in his bed, he was hit with the desperate need to see her face. Grabbing his MacBook off his nightstand, he logged in and pulled up the blog site the promoter of her tour made the girls keep. He expected to see the same goofy pictures she'd had up for a week. But there were new ones.

There was a close-up of her face next to the face of her friend

GIRL ON *Tour* 49

from home—at least that was who he thought it was. Last time he'd seen the girl her hair was white and pink, and now it was black, but he was pretty sure it was the same one. Next there was a picture of Kylie and that young girl on her tour—he couldn't remember her name but her dad was Donovan Taite, a badass producer with serious pull in Nashville, LA, and probably a bunch of other places. Below that photo was a comment from someone named Brett911. He said that it was great to meet all of them tonight, and he'd linked a video he'd posted on YouTube. His profile picture was a bright yellow Porsche and Trace had the sudden urge to punch something. Hard. And to make that trip to the liquor store after all. *Don't be ridiculous, jackass. Calm the hell down.*

Clicking on the link was dangerous. Who the hell knew what it could be? But when he did, he was rewarded with Kylie's beautiful face. It was kind of dark since it was obviously recorded at night, but it was definitely her. She was laughing and grinning at someone next to her. Fuck him if she was looking at some other dude like that. His temples throbbed as he reminded himself of why he'd emptied his place of all hard liquor.

Whoever was filming must've backed up, or zoomed out, and thank God they did. It allowed him to see that it was the black-haired friend from home she was grinning at. They were standing on the tailgate of a jacked up Chevy Silverado. The Taite girl was with them and they were dancing and singing along to one of his songs. His newest. *Rock It on My Tailgate* blared through his speakers, and he couldn't help but shake his head. At least he knew she had to be thinking about him.

Once that song ended, the opening chords of Bryce Parker's *Baby Don't Wait* came on. The girls slowed to match the rhythm of the song. He was struck dumb for a second as Kylie's hips swayed back and forth in a way that nearly undid him. He tried hard to swallow as blood rushed in his ears. Probably because his heart was pounding at the sight of her moving like that. He didn't know if it was the glow of the bonfire in the background lighting her up or if his feelings for her made her shine the way she did, but *good night alive.* He had a feeling it wasn't just him. Whoever was filming—probably Porsche boy—zoomed straight in on *her*. The other girls and the truck disappeared from the frame and the only person visible was Kylie. *His Kylie*, dammit. Brett911 was going to get his fucking face knocked in if Trace ever came across him. Even over the blare of the music he could hear her clear voice singing the lyrics.

So baby don't wait. Don't wait to call me, don't hesitate to show up at my door. Whatever I'm doin', wherever I'm goin', I'd rather be with you more. So baby don't wait.

For once, Bryce Parker got something right. Trace put his computer aside and grabbed his phone off the charger. He pulled up his recent calls and touched her name. This wasn't a text message situation he was dealing with.

"Hullo?" Kylie's sleepy voice answered.

"Hey, pretty girl. Did I wake you?" *Yes you did, dumbass.*

"Mmm, I don't mind. Everything okay?"

No, everything was sure as hell not okay. He could picture her—that messy blond hair spread out on her pillows and her soft, warm, body tangled in the covers. Covers he could hear rustling over the phone. "Just missin' you."

Never in his life had he come straight out and said what he was feeling. Never. Until her.

"Miss you too, Trace."

Oh good Lord, she was trying to kill him. His name on her lips was quite possibly the hottest thing he'd ever heard. Got him every time. "Have a good time tonight?" He clicked off his lamp and settled down into his own covers.

He could hear her smiling as she spoke. "Yeah, it got kinda crazy. But for the most part it was fun. It was good to see Lu."

Who the fuck was Lu? Oh right, her friend from back home. The girl. But what the hell did she mean by *kinda crazy*? His grip on the phone tightened. "Yeah, I'm pretty jealous of Lu right now. And every other asshole who got to watch you up on that tailgate tonight." *Yes, I am stalking you.*

Kylie groaned. "You saw the video then."

He chuckled softly. "Yeah, it was, uh, doing things to me.

Hence the phone call in the middle of the night."

Suddenly her voice sounded much more alert. "Hmm, what kind of *things*, Mr. Corbin?"

Oh, the memories hearing her call him that brought back. Memories of when she hated him and refused to call him by his first name, making him desperate to fuck her hard and rough on every surface of the bus they shared for six torturous and glorious weeks. Not that he'd have been able to fuck the fight out of her. Or the stubbornness. There was always heat between them, at least as far as he was concerned. "Bad things, Kylie Lou. Things not appropriate for your pretty little ears."

"I think my ears, as well as other parts of my body, might be capable of handling a lot more than you think." Her words sent a jolt of electricity shooting straight down his spine to his dick. Her voice had lost its sleepy tenor and was just a sexy whisper, probably meant to keep the other girls on the bus from hearing her. But it was making him so hard it hurt.

"We'll see about that." He didn't have to worry about anyone hearing him, but his laughter was dark and quiet all the same. There was an intimacy about this that he didn't want to mess up. "What are you wearing right now?"

For a second she was quiet, and he hoped he hadn't pissed her off. But when she spoke, her voice was low and thick—rekindling his belief that she needed this as much as he did. "My Hank shirt and panties. Black ones."

"Any chance I can get you to take off the shirt for me?" *Sorry, Hank.*

"Well, now, that depends," she drawled in the sweet Oklahoma accent he loved so much. "What are you going to do for me?"

Oh yeah, this was happening. "What do you want me to do?"

His girl didn't miss a beat. "I want you to touch me, Trace. I *need* you to touch me."

His dick jerked and twitched beneath the covers. He closed his eyes and pictured her there with him. Sliding his hand down, he gripped the thick length of his erection. "Baby, I *need* to touch you so bad. I came damn close to driving to Oklahoma tonight."

She moaned and he almost came right then. "Don't tease me," she pouted.

"Oh I'm not teasing. I have full intentions of pleasing you. In a variety of ways. Until then, how you comin' with that shirt?"

"It's off. Just in panties now." *Thank you Lord for giving me a good imagination.*

"No bra?"

"Nope."

He growled. "Run your hands over those pretty pink nipples for me. Tell me how they feel."

She let a light moan escape. "Hard," she whispered.

"Good. They'd be in my mouth if I was there. Now, run your hand down your stomach, slow. Real slow," he commanded. He gripped his dick harder, willing himself to hold out until he got her off.

"Trace," she whispered. "I don't know if I can do this."

"You can, baby. I'm here. You can, I promise," he reassured her. "Now, rub yourself over those sexy black panties. Tell me how it feels."

"Good. Wet." She whimpered again.

"Mmm, I wish I could be there to taste you. Is it throbbing for me?"

Her voice came out so strained it almost sounded like she was in serious pain. "Y-yes."

"Slide your panties off, Kylie Lou. Kick ' onto the floor."

He could hear her shuffling movements. Good girl was following orders. Lord knew it wasn't something she did normally. He grinned to himself, feeling pretty damn special.

"They're off," she breathed into the phone.

"Spread your legs for me. As far as they can go."

"Can I touch myself?"

Oh sweet Jesus. He loved that she asked permission. He felt himself falling headfirst down towards the point of no return so he removed his hand and tried to pull himself together. He had to take care of his girl first.

"Yeah, you can. Just use one finger at first. Slide it inside for me. Once you're good and wet you can touch your clit, if you're a good girl."

Her heavy breathing was full-on panting when she spoke again. "I'm a good girl. Promise."

He growled into the phone. "Baby, I know you're not alone on that bus, but when I let you come I need to hear you moan my name. Like that night on the bus. Can you do that for me?"

"Yes." She let out a broken whimper and he stroked his cock from tip to bottom and back up again.

"Add another finger, baby. Once they're both nice and wet, rub them over your swollen clit for me." Her breathy moans and whimpers were about to send him over the edge. *Dammit.*

"*Oh God*, Trace."

"Fuck. Come for me, sweet girl."

"N-now?" she stammered.

He knew he couldn't hold back much longer. "Yeah, Kylie Lou. I need you to do it now."

"Okay," she whispered urgently. Son of a motherfucker, he wasn't going to make it. The pressure was building too hard behind the head of his cock as he pictured her touching herself. He was so close. Too close.

She all but screamed out his name and his orgasm burst from the head of his dick.

"*OhgodohgodohTrace*," she moaned in a steady, breathless stream.

He let loose a guttural sound from deep in his chest. "Baby, I'm going to give you a minute to recover while I clean up. Wait for me, okay?"

"Mmhm."

He grinned into the darkness. He knew she couldn't form sentences, or hell, even words after she came.

After he'd done a quick cleanup, he grabbed his phone out of the covers and slid back into his bed. "Now that that's out of the way, how are things?"

She giggled. "Okay, I guess. Be better if you and I were sharing a bus again."

"And yet, we shared a bus for six weeks and you never slept in my bed once."

She scoffed. "That's because you kicked me out of your room."

"Because you were drunk."

"Technicality."

Even in the middle of the night after phone sex she was quick. He was spent, literally, and could barely keep up. He yawned. "I almost forgot. Noel Davies asked about you the other day, about signing you to the label."

"Seriously?"

"Yeah. I think he was fishing for inside info."

"Hmm, did you give him any?"

"I warned him that you were a piece of work and that he wasn't man enough to handle you."

"Trace!" she whisper-yelled at him.

"Naw, I didn't say that. Well, not in so many words. But he did ask if I thought you'd be willing to tour with me for real one day, as in, long term." He wondered if she had any idea how important her response was.

"Long as they keep the bus stocked with enough food so I don't starve. You eat enough for five people."

He laughed out loud, finally breaking the sound barrier between them. "You're the one who kept eating all the bananas."

"Only because you made such a big deal about it."

"Hey, Kylie Lou?"

Now it was her turn to yawn. "Yeah?"

"I really am missing the hell out of you right now. And I hope the tour's going well and no one's giving you a hard time."

"Miss you, too," she said, returning to the soft whisper. Her voice was laced with a sadness he hated. "It's going okay. I can handle it."

"Say the word and I'll come, wherever you are. They can do all this shit without me for a while."

"Are we gonna talk about Gretchen Gibson?" she asked. It was the first time ever—well, no, it was the first time since the first day she'd joined him on his *Back to My Roots* tour—that he'd heard her be timid. Nervous.

"Do we have to?"

"No."

He could practically see her biting her lip. "We will, babe. Promise I'll explain about her and the tour and everything when I've had more sleep."

"Okay," she said quietly.

Subject change needed. Immediately. "Your friend okay, the one who got sick?"

At that, she let out a little laugh, and he felt slightly better about the direction of the conversation. "She fell off that tailgate we were dancing on. Busted her ass."

He laughed. "No shit? Is it on the video?"

"Nah, the guy recording lost interest in us before it happened."

Trace knew better. He'd seen the video. The guy filming had lost interest in everyone else *but* her. She spoke before he could tell her this.

"So, um, have you? Fallen off I mean."

"What? You mean have I been drinking?" He would've been offended, but after what he'd seen of Gretchen and what he knew Kylie had seen of him, it was a pretty fair question. But three beers hardly seemed worth mentioning. No need to stress her out. Especially since he had everything under control and she had enough to deal with. "Naw, babe. I'm good. You shouldn't be worrying about that anyways." This was why he didn't know if what they were doing was a good idea. He was bound to screw up and she was already worrying about him instead of enjoying her own success.

"If you did, you could tell me. I can't say I understand, but I know it can't be easy."

"Get some rest, darlin'. Stop worryin' your pretty little self about me. Night, babe."

"Goodnight, Trace."

CHAPTER Ten

Kylie woke up to the sound of Lily's voice singing one of her obnoxiously perky chart toppers. She'd been deep in a dream involving being very naked with Trace in the pond on his property. She struggled to hold on to the image of them entangled in the water but Lily's voice wouldn't allow it.

"Argh," she grumbled, ambling out of bed.

Betcha wish you woulda called, betcha wish it wasn't too late. Oooh ooh oh now I'm the one walkin' out. Oooh ooh oh, now's who's the one havin' doubts?

The weird part was, it wasn't *actually* Lily singing. It was her voice coming through the speakers in the back of the bus. From Mia's room.

Kylie sidestepped the piles of boots, clothes, and heels strewn in her path and leaned in Mia's doorway. She had to bite her lip to keep from laughing. Mia was straightening her hair in her mirror and singing along with Lily's song blaring from her iPod dock.

Something must have alerted her to Kylie's presence because she jumped, nearly scorching herself with the flat iron. "Christ!"

"Nope, just me." Kylie shrugged. "Didn't realize you were a

fan," she said, nodding to where the music was coming from.

"I'm not," Mia said, reaching over to silence the iPod. "She put that on my iPod this morning. Some of her shit's kind of catchy."

"Did I miss an early morning jam session?"

Mia eyed her up and down. "What? Afraid you're being left out? Can't have that now, can we? God forbid the great *Kylie Ryans* isn't the center of attention for five seconds."

Kylie's cheeks heated at the unexpected burst of hostility. She knew she should probably be used to it by now but for some reason she wasn't. "Pardon me. I was trying to make conversation, trying to act like a professional, or hell, just a decent human being. I can see that you have no idea how to be either of those things so I'm going to give it a rest already."

"Don't you dare talk to me about being a professional or a decent human being," Mia practically growled at her. "You don't know anything about me, do you? Except what you decided the night I showed up at your party."

"Oh but you're the expert on me, right? You know who I'm dating so you know exactly who I am and what I'm about. I have no idea what the hell your problem is. And honestly, I don't even give a shit anymore. You want to be a raging bitch all the time? Knock yourself out. I have more important things to worry about."

Mia smirked, her lips curling into a hateful smile. "Right. Like Skyping your boyfriend to piss and moan about every little thing that doesn't go your way. Or maybe you're just checking in to make sure he still *is* your boyfriend. Or that he's still sober."

Bitch, meet line. 'Cause you just fucking crossed it. Kylie closed her eyes. Her breathing and heart rate were ramped up so high she probably could've mauled Mia Montgomery like a wild bear without breaking a sweat.

She opened her eyes, hoping she'd set the brunette across from her on fire with the blazing heat in them. When she finally spoke, her voice was dead calm. "You can say whatever you like about me. I've been called names you probably don't even know the meaning of. And you can keep throwing your bitchy-ass attitude in my face every time I breathe too close to you if that's what you need to do to be happy. I'll smile. And I might even wink or blow you a kiss. I'm from Oklahoma, honey. I can bless your heart and hate your crazy ass all at the same time. But if you ever, and I mean ever, make another comment about Trace, his drinking or otherwise, then I promise, you won't be able to whistle fucking Dixie when I'm through with you."

She watched as Mia took a step back. Clearly, she'd gotten her point across. So she winked. "Anyways. Lovely chatting with you. As usual. See you at dinner."

She'd been trying so hard not to think about what may or may not have happened with Mia and Trace before she came along. But it was becoming damn near impossible not to wonder.

She was showering when she remembered the text her manager had sent the night before. He'd scheduled a video chat meeting for her with a possible agent. Her late night talk with Trace and the early morning confrontation with Mia had scrambled her brains. She finished up quickly and threw herself together as best she could.

When she made it to the media room, the door was locked. Kylie never even closed it, much less locked it. She checked her phone. It was ten minutes after the time Chaz was supposed to send the video chat request. He was a stickler for punctuality.

"Um? Is there a reason this door's locked?" she called, knocking softly.

"Go away," a muffled voice called back.

Great. "Lily, open the door. I need to use the computer." She took a deep breath. The constant hogging of the bathroom was one thing. But this was affecting her career. She texted Chaz to let him know she wasn't able to get to the computer but was working on it. She knocked again, harder this time. "Seriously. I have a video chat meeting with my manager, like *now*. It's important."

"Use your phone. I'm on the computer right now."

You're always on the damned computer. "My phone has shitty service and a delay. Please, Lily. I promise I'll try to be quick about it."

"God!" Lily shouted as she slid the door open and glared through red-rimmed eyes. "Mia was right about you. You're such a self-centered bitch!"

She didn't even have time to respond before the girl stormed past her. So she screamed at her retreating figure. "I'm self-centered? Seriously? Look in the frickin' mirror sometime! You and Mia can both kiss my self-centered ass!"

With that, she locked herself in the media room. But she didn't call Chaz right away. Instead she sat in the booth and took a few calming breaths, composing herself the best she could. Her phone buzzed. She looked at the text from her manager.

We've been through this. If you're not going to take your career seriously then I won't waste my time. I rescheduled for tomorrow morning at 8am. Don't be late.

She rubbed her hands over her face and fought the urge to cry. Or hit something. Or hit the two other girls on the bus until *they* cried. God. She needed to see Trace's face so bad she could hardly stand it. Needed to see his smile, hear his laugh. The real one, the one that gave her chills and warmed her all at once. Now.

As soon as the window with his handsome face popped up, she smiled. She knew she was probably blushing at the memory of their last conversation. "Hey," she said softly.

"Hey, pretty girl," he greeted her. "Sleep well?"

Just the sound of his deep warm drawl soothed away all of the swirling tension and turmoil inside of her. Kylie bit her lip and tilted her head to the side. "Not as well as I would have if you were here."

She couldn't see them all that clearly through the pixelated image on the computer screen, but she would've bet her Gibson Hummingbird that his eyes were turning that stormy shade of hazel she loved so much.

"Babe, if I was there, you probably wouldn't have slept at all."

She tucked a strand of hair behind her ear and leaned forward, propping her chin on her hand as she did. "I'd be okay with that."

"Kylie! Did you drink the last of the milk?" Mia's voice

interrupted her intimate moment.

Kylie leaned away from the screen and hollered back. "No! The self-centered bitch didn't drink your precious milk. Must've been Lily."

She smiled apologetically into the webcam. "Sorry about that. Things are kind of…" How were things?

"Everything okay?" Trace's forehead creased. No need to bother him with her trivial girl problems.

She waved a hand to let him know it wasn't a big deal. Even though Mia hating her and her wondering why was starting to feel like a very big deal. "Three girls crammed together on a bus is not the best idea ever, you know?"

"Sounds like a great idea to me." Trace winked. She knew he was kidding but it stung a little. He was known for being a ladies' man, and she was currently on tour with someone who may or may not have been one of his prior conquests.

She forced a smile. "Funny."

Trace's mischievous grin faded. "Okay, I'm not a total dumbass. What's going on? You look…mad or worried or…something."

She'd never been one to keep things bottled up. Just as she was opening her mouth to come out and ask him about Mia, Lily stuck her head into the doorway. "Hey, you almost done? My dad's about to call back and my friend Jen is supposed to be Skyping me in like five minutes."

Kylie wanted to tell Lily to catch a damn clue. Her dad rarely made any of their Skype dates or called her back. At least he hadn't since they'd been on tour together. When he did it just provoked a meltdown anyways. Kylie had spent several nights locked out of the bathroom because Lily was shut up in there crying. She'd had to go without a shower more than once because of whatever Lily's dad said or didn't say during their chats. "Be done in a minute," she grumbled.

"Kylie?"

She glanced back at the screen. Trace looked both concerned and irritated. "Yeah, sorry. Lily needs the computer again but—"

"Lily can wait a damn minute. I'm not getting off here until you tell me what the hell is going on."

She glanced up. Thankfully Lily must've decided to let her say goodbye in private. "I need to ask you something. I don't want to, and technically it's none of my business." She pulled in a lungful of air. "But did you and Mia…when you were on tour together, did you—"

"Seriously?" She watched as Trace raked both of his hands through his hair. "Are you going to ask me about every woman I've ever come into contact with? It may not seem like it, but believe it or not, I didn't actually sleep with every single female I met before you."

"Trace…that's not what I was trying to say. It's just, things between me and her are strained and she seems to hate me and I just wanted to know if you'd—"

"Kylie, I really need the computer. *Please.*" Lily was back and she had her whiny voice on.

"One minute," she said, gritting her teeth and glaring at Lily with everything she had.

"I'll tell you what, compile a list and I'll circle the yeses. That work for you?" Even through the computer speaker, he sounded pissed.

"I'll get right on that," she snapped back at him. He'd asked what was wrong and she was trying to tell him and he was being a dick.

She reached up to slam the computer shut, the online equivalent of hanging the fuck up on him, but his expression was apologetic. "Wait. Kylie, please. My bad. I shouldn't have gotten so shitty. It's just, I'm under a lot of pressure right now and things with the tour are crazy." He paused to scrub a hand over his face. "None of that is an excuse for being an asshole to you first thing in the morning. Or ever. Forgive me?"

She rolled her eyes. Only Trace Corbin could make a girl forgive him without ever actually apologizing. "Yeah, I get it. I shouldn't be so—"

"Kylie!" Lily was literally stomping mad.

"Hey, Lily's freaking out and—"

"Yeah, I hear. Look, this isn't exactly the kind of conversation we need to have on here anyways but I'll see you in a week in Nashville. Okay?"

She smiled and the tightness in her chest loosened slightly. *One more week.* It couldn't come soon enough. "Okay. Call me later if you get a chance. I know you're busy."

"I will. Miss you, Kylie Lou."

"Miss you, too."

"Finally," Lily blurted out, practically shoving Kylie out of her seat.

Kylie left the media room feeling more than a little agitated. For one, Lily was driving her nuts. And for two, Mia was lingering beside the doorway, smirking her ass off as Kylie passed. She wondered how much she'd overheard.

Just the sight of the girl reminded her of what was bothering her more than anything. Even more than Lily's rudeness or fighting with Mia.

Trace hadn't ever answered her question.

CHAPTER Eleven

"I can't help but notice the few stops on the tour that you were insistent on just happen to coincide with the tour of another artist we're familiar with," Pauly said as they loaded their luggage onto the bus.

Trace raised a brow. "Really? I hadn't noticed."

His manager laughed. "Sure you hadn't."

So maybe he hadn't been all that discreet. Just because he and Kylie were keeping their relationship quiet didn't mean he was going to spend twelve or more weeks without her. He made sure they'd meet up in Nashville both times she was there, plus Atlanta and Charlotte. Even Gretchen's crazy ass being banned from the Atlanta Amphitheater hadn't been able to screw up his plans. He'd made a few calls and begged favors from some guys he knew from back home. His ass was on the line now, and if Gretchen caused any problems in Georgia, he was going to strangle her with his bare damn hands.

Once they were finished, Trace wiped the sweat from his brow. He loved outdoor shows. This was what he'd always wanted and never could get the label to go for. Finally he'd been able to convince them to let him do it his way. And the bastards had strapped Gretchen to him like a time bomb. They knew she was unstable—hell, everyone knew. He had a feeling that was exactly what they were hoping for. For one or both of them to screw up and give them an excuse to drop them both, scraping them off the bottom of their shoes like dog shit.

Well, he was a new man. Okay, maybe not entirely. But he was working on it. He was meeting with Dr. Reynolds regularly and calling him when he felt the urge to drink. Well, when he got the urge to get shitfaced anyways. He also had him joining them on several tour stops so that he and Mike, his bass player who was also a recovering alcoholic, could have private AA meetings with him. His girlfriend and his sisters deserved better than the man he'd been for the past few years. He was going to make damn sure they got better.

Gretchen, on the other hand—he couldn't speak for. As soon as Pauly stepped away to take a phone call, Trace heard it. The sound of someone retching her brains out. It was coming from inside the bus. He stepped on and headed towards the bathroom.

"Wow, Gretchen. You couldn't make it one day?" He watched as she finished heaving into the toilet.

"Shut it, Corbin." She moaned. She flushed the toilet and stood, wiping her mouth as she turned to face him. "You should've gone out with us after the launch party last night. You used to be so much more fun." She tried to pout at him but her eyes were bloodshot and she reeked of alcohol and vomit.

"Yeah, looked like you were having tons of fun in there," he said with a nod towards the bathroom. "Sorry I missed it."

"Are you going to be this uptight for the entire tour? Because if you are, I'm going to need a lot more alcohol."

"If by uptight you mean am I going to expect you to stay conscious on stage each night? Then yeah, I guess I am." He shrugged, but inside he was feeling a little sick himself. They hadn't even left Nashville and Gretchen was already messed up.

No way they were going to make it sixteen weeks on the road together. He was starting to get an idea of exactly how his girlfriend had felt a few months ago when she'd joined his screwed-up self on tour.

Watching as Gretchen sauntered off the bus, a feeling he was familiar with seeped into his skin. The same feeling he had when his mom or Claire Ann sported a black eye or an armful of fingerprint bruises courtesy of his piece of shit father. Because he hadn't been able to do anything to stop it. There was nothing he hated more than feeling powerless. Helpless. He was disgusted with himself. Completely and utterly disgusted.

Memories he'd tried to drink away flooded his mind. The yelling. The crying. Rae—tiny and terrified—hiding under the kitchen table. The way he'd once grabbed Kylie by the arm the exact same way his father used to grab the women he supposedly "loved."

Stop. It's over. In the past. You're nothing like him…except, you're pretty much exactly like him. He tried to focus on his breathing but his chest ached and his head began to throb. His fists clenched and he darted into his room. In the dresser was still one last bottle of his favorite bourbon, Heaven Hill. *Thank God.*

CHAPTER Twelve

As she stepped off the bus to walk to the restaurant where the meeting with Brian Miller was, Kylie checked her phone. She'd been planning to send Trace a good luck message because his tour was kicking off that night in Alabama and they hadn't exactly ended their last conversation on the best note. But the two texts she'd already received stopped her cold.

One was from Lulu. **Saw the article online. Everything okay?** The other was from Tonya, a friend she'd made waitressing back in Nashville. **Hey hon. Heard you and Trace are having a hard time. Hang in there. Long distance relationships can be tough.**

What the hell? She pulled up the web browser on her phone and did the one thing Trace had told her never to do. She Googled herself.

COUNTRY COUPLE UPDATE: IS THE HONEYMOON ALREADY OVER FOR CORBIN AND HIS LATEST FLING?

She clicked the link and read the few lines talking about her and Trace. Her vision blurred but she could read the main points. *All they do is argue, says a source close to Ryans.* She scrolled down the screen. There was more. For a second, everything was tinged in red. They'd had one minor disagreement since being apart. Over Mia, who'd been listening in on her conversation. She'd put up with the crazy chick being cold and distant and sometimes downright hateful. But this was bullshit. And Kylie intended to tell her so.

Below that was a link to another article. One that almost caused her to forget about the situation with Mia entirely. Almost.

TROUBLED ARTISTS TRACE CORBIN & GRETCHEN GIBSON CELEBRATE THEIR UPCOMING CO-HEADLINING TOUR WITH A NIGHT OUT ON THE TOWN.

She couldn't even read the article because she was too distracted by the pictures. Her surroundings began to spin as bile rose in her throat. Her stomach clenched and her entire body tingled with a painful intensity similar to what she imagined being electrocuted would feel like.

Struggling to swallow, she clicked on the album featuring the grainy photos of Trace and Gretchen. The first showed him checking her out while they played pool. The next one was of the woman licking Trace's neck as they took body shots off one another. With each click Kylie's heart pounded harder. Her hands trembled as she swallowed the lump in her throat and stared at the image of Trace holding Gretchen in his arms on the dance floor in the middle of a bar.

There has to be an explanation. There has to be. She just hoped it wasn't something along the lines of he was out having a good time, getting wasted with Gretchen Gibson, like he'd be doing for the entirety of his tour. Even though that was exactly what it looked like.

Her mood had gone from bad to emotionally unstable on a nuclear level by the time they made it to dinner. She got that Mia wouldn't be heading up her fan club any time soon. She could deal with that. But leaking her personal information to the press was low. For anyone. And Kylie had enough issues without her adding to them.

Mia's eyes fell on her a few times during dinner, and her

expression said she didn't miss the fact that Kylie wasn't speaking to her. Not directly anyways. The tables had turned. After Kylie blatantly rolled her eyes at something Mia had said, the other girl threw her arms up. "Feel free to share with the group, Oklahoma. What the hell is your problem?" Mia leaned forward, eyed Kylie, and took a sip of her beer.

"Um, I think I covered everything," Brian Miller said as he stood. "Text me if you have any questions."

Once he was out of the way, Kylie met Mia's glare. "I'm not the one with a problem. You're the one running your mouth all over town about my personal business."

The brunette smirked. "What *personal* business are you talking about? Because honestly, I have zero interest in what goes on between you and your precious boyfriend."

"That's funny. Rumor has it you were once interested in making him *your* boyfriend." Kylie tried to keep her voice down but a few women at a nearby table glanced over. Referring to Trace as anyone's boyfriend out loud felt weird. She didn't have time to analyze why.

"Guys, seriously. This is dumb. Please don't do this. Not here." Lily tried to lean between them but Mia scooted her chair forward, effectively blocking the petite girl from interrupting.

"No," Mia began, "I want to hear this. What's this *rumor* you speak of?" Her green eyes gleamed with angered interest and Kylie fought the urge to back down. She didn't know if she wanted to know this. She still hadn't come right out and demanded an answer from Trace because she knew the truth might make touring with Mia even more awkward than it already was. But it was kind of late now.

"You didn't leave Trace's *Back to My Roots* tour because of *personal issues,* did you? You left because you…" Lord, she did not want to say this out loud. She lowered her voice to barely above a whisper. "You left because you hooked up with Trace and he didn't—"

"Whoa," Mia interrupted, her face contorted by shock. "Excuse the fuck out of you. No, I damn sure did not 'hook up with Trace.'

That's your story darlin', not mine."

"But Pauly said—"

"You know what? Screw this. I'm going back to the bus." Mia stood and turned to leave at the exact moment the waiter arrived with more drinks. Kylie shoved her chair back to follow her and bumped him, causing the entire tray to tilt. She felt the liquid splashing over her and looked up just in time to see that Mia had received the worst of it. *Wonderful.* Kylie turned and saw that the ladies at the table next to them were using their camera phones to record the whole thing.

"Mia, wait!" She ran out of the restaurant, nearly tripping over her heels.

"Kylie," Lily called after her. But she didn't stop. She had just accused Mia of something that apparently wasn't true and she hated people who went around doing that. Now she was one of them. And damn, Mia Montgomery could *move.*

When she finally reached the bus, she was panting. Lily clomped on behind her and they walked to Mia's door. Which was shut. And locked. Kylie knocked softly.

"Mia?"

Nothing.

"Mia, can we talk, please? Like civilized people instead of high school girls who make asses of themselves in the cafeteria?"

Still nothing. Kylie looked over her shoulder at Lily, who shrugged. She took a deep breath. "Mia, I'm sorry for what I said. I had no right to accuse you of that. It's just, Pauly said something and it's been bugging me and I know I should've—"

She was interrupted by Mia sliding the door open. The girl glared at her as she pulled on a dry T-shirt. "You should've what? Asked me if I screwed your boyfriend before accusing me of it?" Kylie flinched but Mia wasn't done. "Maybe you should've asked before deciding that I've been leaking your *personal business* online, too, which I haven't, by the way. Either of those things." She leaned in the doorway and folded her arms.

Kylie felt the relief at Mia's declarations, both of them, flooding through her chest. "Okay. Well, good. And you're right, I should have. But honestly, you've been grinding an ax over my head since day one. Look, I was a bitch at my party but I was hurting and I jumped to conclusions. The wrong ones, apparently. And then you act like you hate us most of the time and yet suddenly you and Lily are thick as thieves. But I'm still on the receiving end of the glares and the smirks and the silent treatment. You're the only ones who could possibly know about what Trace and I have said in our conversations and—"

"It wasn't her that leaked that stuff," Lily said softly, causing both Mia and Kylie to turn and look at her. "It was me."

Kylie's eyes went round and wide. She felt her face go hot but she held back. She knew she didn't need to make another scene like she had with Mia. "Okay. Mind telling me why you would do that?"

Lily's eyes began to fill with tears as she looked up from underneath her eyelashes. "I didn't mean to, Kylie, I swear. I was talking to my friend Jen from back home earlier. I was complaining because my dad had promised to call me but you were on there with Trace and I made a comment about how y'all were always arguing on there lately. I wasn't thinking. I promise I didn't mean for her to go tell people that. I forgot I even said it. And then my dad never called and I…" She trailed off, very obviously choking over her shame.

Kylie was equal parts pissed off and sympathetic. Lily's dad was clearly an ass who could care less about his daughter. She'd learned enough already as she watched Lily sit around waiting for him to call, or show up at a concert, or Skype her, to know that he hardly bothered. Guess he thought throwing money at her and paying to send her on tour to keep her busy would be good enough. And the girl obviously felt bad. Really bad. She was always so annoyingly perky that seeing her so defeated and upset was disturbing.

Kylie took a deep breath and shook her head. "It's okay. I mean—it's not *okay* okay. And in the future, it would be awesome if you kept your mouth shut about anything to do with me. This is bigger than us and people can use me to cause problems for Trace."

"I'm sorry. About earlier too. I really am."

As much as Kylie wanted to stay mad, she just didn't have it in her. She'd used up all her energy on Mia. "It's fine. Forget about it. I have."

Lily nodded, her small, pink mouth turning down at the corners as she retreated to her room.

"Well, aren't you just little Miss Congeniality?" Mia snorted. "When it was me, you were on a rampage, but Princess Lily runs her mouth and all is forgiven. Nice."

Kylie closed her eyes and tried to gather herself. "You know what, Mia? Why don't you just say whatever it is you want to say to me so we can move on?"

The other girl's eyes narrowed. "That really what you want?"

Kylie's heart pounded in her chest. Was it? She wasn't sure. But she couldn't take any more of the unadulterated hatred constantly coming at her either. "Yeah, it is," she confirmed.

Mia licked her lips and swallowed hard. "I think you got where you are because of who you're dating. I think you'd step over anyone who got in your way to be the next big thing."

Kylie recoiled, feeling the sting of the words as if she'd been slapped. She didn't say anything as Mia closed the door in her face. For once, she didn't have anything to say.

Because everything she said is true.

CHAPTER Thirteen

"Thank you, Birmingham! Y'all are beautiful!" After two encores, Trace exited the stage at the Oak Mountain Amphitheater and headed back towards the bus. Gretchen was closing the first show and he couldn't have been happier. He'd waited all day to talk to Kylie, and then she'd canceled their Skype date because of a meeting with the guy helping them with their tour site stuff. She didn't have a show tonight so he'd promised to call her as soon as he was done performing.

Once he'd thanked the guys and chatted with Mike a bit to make sure he was hanging in there, he hopped on the bus and grabbed his phone.

"Hey." She sounded tired and kind of like she'd been crying.

"Hey, baby. Everything okay?"

"Oh yeah. Everything's wonderful." Her tone was laced with something lethal. Anger. She was angry. But she was playing it off for some reason.

"Doesn't sound wonderful. You and the girls gettin' along?"

"Not really. You and *Gretchen* gettin' along?" Oh shit. That did not sound good. She said Gretchen's name like it burned in her mouth.

"Er, I guess so. I mostly avoid her. She's...got some issues."

Kylie snorted out a harsh laugh. "Really? From what I saw, it doesn't look like you're avoiding her at all."

"Um, babe, I don't know what you think you've seen but Gretchen and I—"

"You listen to me, Trace Corbin. Don't you dare talk to me like I'm some naïve idiot who doesn't know what she's seen. Please go suck it up and Google your fucking self." With that, she hung up. Actually hung the hell up on him. Well this night was going downhill fast. She knew good and well he had a strict rule about not ever looking himself up online. He forbade his sisters from doing it too. He'd advised her to do the same. Because people were assholes. The anonymity of the Internet really tended to bring out the inner asshole in some. But his girl was upset about something she'd seen and he had to know what it was. As soon as he got a drink.

His hands shook as he poured himself a few inches of dark liquid in a plastic cup. He made a point to screw the lid back on the bottle. This was it. Just enough to take the edge off, to slow the adrenaline coursing through him.

He pulled out his laptop and tried to log onto the Internet. Apparently the backside of a mountain in Alabama wasn't a great service area. He didn't even want to imagine what she'd seen about him and Gretchen.

He closed his eyes and tried to think. He knew one girl who was always online and generally made a habit of knowing more than she should. Plus he missed her and wanted to hear her voice. So he finished his drink, savoring the slow, sweet burn while he pulled her number up on his phone. She picked up on the first ring. He held the phone a little ways away from his ear in anticipation of her squealing.

"Trace! I was just thinking about you!" Yep, there was squealing. Good thing he'd been prepared.

"Hey, baby girl. You missin' me?"

"You know I am!" He could practically see her beautiful smile.

The same one that had wrapped him around her little finger the first time he'd ever seen it.

"I miss you too, Rae. But I'm actually calling because Kylie's upset with me and—"

His little sister, who, much to his dismay wasn't so little anymore, interrupted him. "Oh no! Why?"

"Because I'm practically an expert in the art of pissing off women."

Rae laughed softly. "Nah, you make me pretty happy. I'm still loving my car by the way."

Trace grinned despite the heap of trouble he was in at the moment. "You're wearing your seatbelt and not texting and driving, right?"

"Yes, *Dad*."

An ice-cold hand plunged into his chest and squeezed. He wished he *had* been her dad instead of the sorry fucker they'd been stuck with. May his black soul not rest in peace. But he was ten years older than her, so he was the closest thing she had. Just the thought of the man had him pouring himself another drink. "Rae, I need you to Google me. Please."

"But you said never to—"

"I know what I said. But Kylie's really upset and I have no idea what I've done this time." He used the hand not holding his phone to rub his temples. This was not how he usually celebrated the end of a kickass show.

"Just a sec," she said. He stood up and paced a path around the bus while he waited for her response. "Okay, you ready for this?"

No. "Yeah, tell me what came up." He eyed the bottle sitting on top of his dresser. He'd barely even broken the neck of it. *See? All under control.*

He heard the girl take a deep breath. "Um, so there's like three articles about you and Gretchen hooking up and having a night out on the town. The rest of the links look like just tour info. But on the images…"

"What about the images? Tell me."

"The first one is of you and Gretchen Gibson taking body

shots off of each other. The second is of you staring at her like an obsessed creeper while she plays pool. And the third is of you dancing together in a bar."

Jesus Mary Mother. Some asshole had used the photo shoot pictures to make it look like he and Gretchen were involved. And out drinking together. No wonder Kylie Lou was so beside herself. He unscrewed the cap on his bourbon and took a swig straight from the bottle without even consciously meaning to.

He swallowed and took a deep breath. "Okay, we are going to discuss how you even know what body shots are at a later date. For now, please tell Claire Ann that it was a promotional photo shoot for the tour and that there was water in my shot glass if she sees them. I gotta go, baby girl. I love you."

"Love you, too. Good luck with Kylie."

"Thanks." *I'm damn sure gonna need it.*

CHAPTER Fourteen

"Stop looking at them." Lily demanded as she slammed the computer screen closed.

"Hey!" Kylie protested, flipping the screen back up. "I might have been checking my email or posting on the blog."

"No you weren't. You were looking at those pictures. I could tell by the look on your face."

"They were promos for the tour, he said." She bit her lip. He'd called back and explained. She knew she needed to get a grip. It was just easier said than done.

"Whatever. I need the computer. My dad should be calling any second." Lily plopped down next to her in the booth.

"Okay." Kylie swallowed the lump that looking at the photos of Trace and Gretchen Gibson taking body shots off of each other had caused.

"Is she looking at them again?" Mia asked, poking her head into the media room and smirking at Kylie. *She's probably enjoying this.*

"Jesus. Can a girl not check her Facebook?" Kylie shook her head and stood. "I'm done, okay? Y'all can use the computer all you want."

Mia stepped aside to let her out of the cramped room. "You'll see him next week, right? He's coming to the show, isn't he?"

Is she trying to comfort me or does she want to see him as much as I do?

Kylie took a few deep breaths and tried to keep her voice calm. "Yeah, his show in Louisville is in the afternoon, and he should make it to the music festival by the time I go on. Long as y'all are still okay with me closing."

Both girls nodded. Their expressions were matching masks of sympathy. Mia's was tinged with disgust. Or pity. Or maybe amusement. Kylie wanted to scream. She'd have preferred they both go back to being bitchy.

"I'm going to bed." She sulked to her room, semi-grateful that Lily had interrupted her. The CMA Music Festival where she'd be performing seemed a million miles away. He'd called right back after she'd acted like a childish idiot. She believed him about the photos. But it still hurt. Bad. She texted him goodnight, knowing he was probably asleep or busy. She lay awake for a long time, waiting for a text back. Just something that connected them. It had almost been six weeks since they'd been together on his farm in Macon. When she looked at the pictures of him and Gretchen, she couldn't help but feel like she'd dreamed the whole thing.

Because when she closed her eyes, the images of Trace and a dark-haired woman drinking together, dancing, playing pool—looking for all the world like they were out on a date and having a hell of a time—flashed behind her eyes. She'd stared at them for so long they were burned into her retinas.

The next morning started with a Lily Taite breakdown of epic proportions. It was nearly enough to make Kylie forget all about the pictures of her boyfriend with another woman. Almost.

"Lily? Lily, come on. We're gonna be late." Kylie sighed as she watched Mia banging on the bathroom door. She leaned against the counter—at least she thought there was a counter under all the curling irons, shoes, clothes, and piles of makeup.

Kylie couldn't even count which number breakdown this was. Once again, Lily had locked her crazy ass in the bathroom with her cellphone and was refusing to come out.

Mia knocked again. They'd been with Lily a few short weeks and they both knew her dad wasn't going to show up for shit. Yet Lily was sixteen-years-old, had been dealing with him her whole life, and still didn't seem to get it.

Kylie stepped towards the bathroom door. "Listen, Lil, we're supposed to meet with Brian at that little diner so he can show us how to post videos and stuff to the site before tonight's show."

"I don't care." Lily's muffled voice came from the other side of the door. "Just go on. I'm not going to post any stupid videos anyways."

"Lily," Mia began in her calmest voice. "This is part of our contract, remember? This isn't something you can just stop doing because you're having a bad day, okay?"

Kylie watched as Mia fumed at the door. She was a no-nonsense chick and Lily was practically made of nonsense.

"Go away!" Lily screamed.

"Listen to me!" Mia yelled right back. "Get your spoiled little ass out here and come the fuck on. Grow the hell up, Lily. You wanted this, wanted to be on this tour. So you are damn well on it. Now let's go!" Mia smacked the door hard with her hand. Kylie winced. That was going to leave a mark.

And it didn't work. Lily's sobs got louder. Kylie shrugged at Mia. "Maybe we should just tell Brian she isn't feeling well."

"Right, let's start making excuses for her like everyone else does. Great idea."

Lily's pampered princess act pissed her off too. But she also felt kind of sorry for her. If her daddy was still alive, she knew he'd put on his one dress shirt—the gray striped one he wore to weddings, funerals, and the few times they went to church—and come to every show of hers he could. A flicker of anger began to well up in Kylie's gut. What the hell was Lily's dad's deal? Could he not be bothered to show his daughter a tiny bit of support or affection? Far as she'd seen, he hadn't shown up for anything and his few calls left Lily in tears.

The night Lily had fallen off the tailgate in Oklahoma, she'd gotten wasted and cried and gone on about her dad not paying enough attention to her. Kylie had chalked it up to the alcohol. But she could see there was more to it. Lily had been all over several random guys at the party. Kylie practically had to drag her off of them and out of there. Girl might as well have had a neon sign flashing 'Daddy Issues' over her head. Lord help if *Country Weekly* ever found out about that.

She sucked in a breath and leaned past Mia towards the door again. "Lily, please come out so we can talk. You don't have to go to dinner with us. I'll see if Brian will write down the instructions. Or email them or something. Okay?"

Kylie heard shuffling and then the door opened. Lily looked like she'd been punched in the face. More than once. Kylie struggled to keep her shock from showing. After taking a deep breath, she stepped towards Lily, who clutched her phone like a lifeline. "Lil, why don't you just tell us what happened? It'll make you feel better to talk about it." She didn't know if this was true. She personally *hated* talking about her problems. But she and Lily were different that way.

"H-he," she began, cutting herself off with a sob. The girl who usually seemed full of life and obnoxious energy suddenly seemed extremely small and weak. "He went to California. Said he had business to handle at his LA office. But really he was just at my brother's soccer game instead of coming to see my show." She held up her phone as evidence.

Kylie and Mia both leaned in to see the Facebook photo of an extremely good looking soccer player with his arm around an older man in a dress shirt who must've been Donovan Taite. Nice. He could fly across the country to see one kid kick a ball around, but he couldn't drive five minutes up the road to see his daughter perform for hundreds of people? What the hell was this guy's problem? Obviously he wasn't a shitty dad to his son. Lily might be annoying but she was a sweet girl who worked hard. Kylie had a nagging suspicion she was working hard specifically to impress a dad who obviously didn't think she was worth her weight in salt. Well…someone certainly needed a talking to.

CHAPTER Fifteen

"*Hey*. You busy?"

Trace tried to sound calmer than he was. "Never too busy for you, babe. What's up?"

"What do you know about Donovan Taite?" Kylie asked, catching him off guard.

"As in *The* Donovan Taite? The CEO of BackRoom Records?"

"That's the one."

He took a deep breath before answering. "Not much. Never met him. Isn't his daughter on tour with you?"

"Yeah. And he's a dick. I was wondering if you knew where exactly in Nashville his office was."

"Jesus, Kylie. You can't go around calling men like Donovan Taite a dick. I mean, you can, but I wouldn't recommend it. At least not where anyone can hear you."

"Oh, I'm going to make sure people hear me all right. Mainly *him*."

He pressed a hand to his forehead as he tried to figure out a way to shake some sense into his hot mess of a girlfriend over the phone. "Please listen to me, Hothead. This is not a man *I'd* mess with. He's got the kind of connections that come from knowing members of the mob, if you get what I'm saying. He not only creates artists, he destroys them. To the point where you never hear of them again, ever. Do not, Kylie, I repeat, do not go screwing around with anything involving him."

Kylie's voice was low when she responded. "He doesn't show up to anything of hers, Trace. He doesn't return her calls. He flies across the country to see his son but can't so much as pick up the phone to tell Lily he's proud of her. Does he have an office in Nashville or not?"

Gretchen moaned loudly before he could respond. She was wailing like an animal in pain with her head on the table as he carried the vomit-covered bed sheets past her on his way to the dumpster. She'd nearly drunk herself to death the night before and she was paying for it now. Part of him wished he'd just minded his own business. But he'd been there. So he was helping her the best he could. Even though he was slightly hungover himself. He balanced his phone on his shoulder. "Yeah, but you shouldn't go there. Listen, I know you. I can tell you're upset and I'm sure whatever Donovan Taite has done is shitty enough to deserve your anger. But he's not a man you mess with."

"I just want to talk to him. Just want to tell him what he's doing to his daughter is wrong. If my daddy was alive, armed guards wouldn't be able to keep him from my shows. She's...she's not okay, Trace. I can't just sit back and watch him break her."

He heaved the disgusting pile of bedclothes into the dumpster. "I hear you, babe. I do. But I'm not kidding. Promise me you won't—"

Fuck. As he released the last of the acidic smelling sheets into the dumpster, his phone fell from his ear. When he picked it up the screen was shattered to hell. Kylie had told him to get one of those cases that kept it safe even if a tank backed over it, but had he? Why hell no. And now the damn thing was dead and wouldn't turn back on. And for all he knew, his girlfriend was going to walk her hotheaded ass straight into a lion's den with a T-bone slung around her neck. Fucking Gretchen. He kicked the dumpster just before pitching his phone into it.

"What the hell's your problem?" Watery bloodshot eyes glared at him as he slammed a travel-size mug of coffee down on the table in front of Gretchen.

"My problem is that you're ruining my damned life. My problem is that if I hadn't been here last night, you'd be fucking dead." Trace took a breath to keep from screaming at the woman. He folded his arms and leaned against the counter. The counter that reminded him of his sexy-ass girlfriend sitting on top of it with her legs spread to accommodate him. *Focus, dammit.* "My problem, Gretchen, is that you're not holding up your end of the deal here. I'm working my ass off to prove that I can do this. That I deserve this last shot that Capital has given me. And you're doing your best to ruin it every step of the way."

Yeah, he saw the damned irony. He'd paid attention in tenth grade English. Mostly because his teacher had some fine-ass legs. But he'd heard a few things she'd said too. God love Kylie for seeing the good in him even when he was behaving like this. He wanted to throttle Gretchen, throw her ass off the bus, and tell Carl to step on it. Looking at her, he couldn't imagine what in the hell Kylie Ryans saw in him. He rubbed his eyes.

Gretchen was still glaring at him when he stopped. "I forgot, you're Mr. Perfect now. Mr. Talks-to-His-Addiction-Specialist-When-He-Has-a-Moment-of-Weakness. Good for fucking you. Just don't forget, you're also Mr. Punched-Out-Several-Guys-Who-Didn't-Deserve-It, Screwed-Anything-That-Moved, and wait, isn't your girlfriend like fifteen? How's your mom, by the way?"

He'd never wanted a drink so badly in his life. His chest tightened as the intensity of his need nearly overtook him. He'd bet Gretchen had a stash of liquor bottles in her room. His was empty. His fists clenched. He dropped them to his sides and flexed his fingers while counting to ten. And then twenty…five. He blew out a breath and lowered himself into the booth where she sat. "You're right, Gretch. I'm an asshole. And Kylie's nineteen, not that it's any of your business. She's still more of a grown up than I am on my best day."

Gretchen's expression said she wasn't interested in hearing about his girlfriend. Or anything else he had to say. "Sounds like a real prize. Congratulations," she deadpanned.

"And you know good and well my mom doesn't want shit to do with me. So whatever you're trying to do here, it won't work." He tilted his head. Gretchen Gibson was a bitch. But she was like him in a lot of ways. Defensive. Angry. Weak when it came to opportunities to numb the pain. But what pain was she numbing? He had no clue. Didn't particularly care to know.

"I'm not trying to *do* anything. Why don't you just do your thing and I'll do mine? Feel free to mind your owned damned business." Her eyes narrowed to cat-like slits.

"We're on tour together. Whether we like it or not, what you do affects me. And your *thing* is going to get you killed, Gretch. Or at the very least get both of us sacked from Capital before you can order your next tequila sunrise. You need help." *I'm one to talk.* Yeah, he felt like a hypocrite. But their situations were completely different. He had his drinking under control. He wasn't out getting trashed like Gretchen, sleeping around, or passing out in his own vomit.

"Go to hell," she hissed, standing abruptly. He watched helplessly as she stormed back to her room. Dropping his head into his hands, he focused on the reasons why he shouldn't drink. *Kylie deserves better. So does Claire Ann. And Rae. I've worked too hard to throw my career away like this. I sure as shit don't want to end up like Gretchen.* And repeat.

But it was still there. That want. The need to swallow shot after shot until he couldn't think about the trouble Kylie was getting into with Donovan Taite or the fucked up mess that was Gretchen Gibson. And worst of all, the fact that just like when he was a kid living under the roof of a volatile man who used his fists instead of words, he was powerless to do anything about any of it.

Chapter Sixteen

"Got a minute?" Mia's head poked into her room and Kylie braced herself for the blast of shit that was probably about to follow.

"Sure. What did I do this time? Wait, don't tell me. Just say whatever bitchy thing you came to say." She leaned back and waited.

Mia swallowed hard and took a step inside. "I didn't come to say anything bitchy. Believe it or not I came to apologize. What I said about Trace, that's none of my business. It wasn't a fair comment to make and I shouldn't have made it."

What about all of the other unfair comments?

"Okay. I shouldn't have accused you of the things I accused you of. So I guess we're even." Kylie stared at her, waiting for the fallout. The 'but I still hate you for breathing' part.

"So um, anyways…I was going to head into town, stop by my apartment, and maybe grab—"

"Hey, can I come with? I have a pit stop to make downtown."

Mia's brow furrowed. *She probably doesn't want me to know where she lives.* Not that Kylie could really blame her since she had technically threatened her with violence. "I guess. You ready now?"

Kylie nodded. She'd just gotten her first shower in two days since Lily had *finally* come out of the bathroom. She was past ready.

When the two of them arrived at the corporate offices of BackRoom Records, Mia freaked. Rightly so. "Are you insane? This isn't the time or place to make a scene, Oklahoma."

"We're not going to make a scene, Mia. We're just going to talk to him. Relax."

The girl sighed as she walked through the door Kylie held open. "Okay, but for the record, this was your idea and I just came along in case you got arrested."

"Fine." The two girls rode the elevator up to the twenty-seventh floor. When they stepped out into the immaculate reception area, Mia let out a low whistle.

Kylie stepped up to the blonde at the reception desk, trying her best not to be intimidated by the impressive office area. "Kylie Ryans, here to see Donovan Taite."

The woman barely looked up. "Is he expecting you?"

"Probably not," Kylie said with a shrug. "But it's important. It's about his daughter."

"Have a seat," the woman said, eyeing Kylie's jeans and tattered Rum Room T-shirt. She knew she probably looked like a waitress, but oh the hell well. Five minutes ago she *was* a waitress, dammit. No shame in her game. Blondie could deal.

"Actually I need to see him immediately. We have a performance tonight that we can't be late for. What I have to say won't take long." She was probably only staying long enough for Mr. Taite to call security anyways.

The receptionist narrowed her eyes. "Miss Ryans, was it?"

Kylie nodded.

"Mr. Taite has an extremely high profile client list. He's a very busy man, and while I'm sure he can hardly wait to hear what you have to say, anyone wanting to see him makes an appointment."

"I see. Well, how about you just do me a favor and do your *one* job and press that intercom button to let him know I'm here to speak with him about his daughter. Lily. Might want to use her name incase he's forgotten it. If he doesn't want to see me, I'll go." *Lord, please don't strike me down for lyin'.*

The woman glared so hard that Mia took a step back. But Kylie stayed rooted where she stood, the image of Lily clutching her phone like a live grenade still fresh in her mind.

The two of them watched as the woman pressed the intercom button and informed the almighty Mr. Taite that a *Miss. Ryans* was here to see him about his daughter. There was a brief pause before he said, "Send her on back, Julie."

The receptionist jerked her head towards a door at the end of the hall.

"Thanks so much, *Julie*," Kylie drawled, pulling Mia along with her.

"You have a real way with people, you know that?" Mia huffed under her breath.

"It's a gift," Kylie answered. Her hands began to tremble. Lily's drunken voice blabbering about her daddy not caring about her, about her not being good enough, about trying so hard to make him proud, to make him notice, was on a steady loop playing through her head. Mia hadn't seen anything yet.

She jerked the heavy mahogany door open and Mia followed close behind. Donovan Taite looked up from his desk. He was handsome for a guy probably in his late forties or early fifties. Not that it mattered.

"Mr. Taite," Kylie said as she marched up to his desk. "I'm Kylie Ryans and this is Mia Montgomery. We're currently on tour with your daughter—"

"Ryans? The waitress? The one shacking up with Trace Corbin as he goes down in flames?" His forehead wrinkled as he looked up at her.

Well, now she really hated him. "No, sir." She forced her best smile. "Ryans, the one who is soon to be topping the charts over all of your clients. Ryans, the one who worked her ass off to get here. And for today, Mr. Taite, Ryans, the one who's about to give you a detailed description of what your sorry-ass excuse for parenting skills are doing to your daughter." Whew. Kylie exhaled. It felt good to get that out of the way.

Mr. Taite raised a brow. "My daughter?"

"Yeah, you know. She's about five two, blond, sixteen, and touring around the country instead of being in high school. We call her Lily, but you obviously can't be bothered to call her at all." Adrenaline pumped hard and fast through her body. She prayed she wasn't shaking visibly.

At that, Donovan Taite stood. Jesus, he was tall. And had a huge booming voice to match. "Now wait just a damned minute—"

"No, Mr. Taite, you wait a damned minute. For two months we've watched her call you, only to be told you're too busy to talk. Watched her sit in front of the computer, waiting for Skype dates that never happened. And if you really want to know—we've also watched her drink herself into oblivion while blubbering like a baby about a daddy who doesn't think she's good enough to be his daughter."

The man opened his mouth to speak but Kylie wasn't done. "And for the record, she's pretty damned talented, despite the fact that she's really just in the music business to get your attention. Not that you would know. Or care."

"Easy, Oklahoma," Mia whispered from behind her. "Maybe take it down a notch."

The man eyed her up and down. "I didn't know you were part of the tour Lily was on. Certainly if I'd known she was associating with a girl like you, I would've reconsidered allowing her to go."

By *a girl like you* he meant trash. Kylie could see in his eyes that was how he perceived her. Fine by her. He was nothing but a grade A asshole in a suit as far as she was concerned. "Well how the hell would you know who she's on tour with? You can't be bothered to take five minutes out of your busy schedule to see her perform."

He sat back down as if he'd grown bored with the whole thing. "Miss Ryans, I think that's about enough. Please let yourself out so I don't have to call security."

Mia tugged at her arm but Kylie didn't move. "Did you go to California to see your son play soccer?"

"Excuse me? What I do is none of your—"

Kylie raised her voice. "Did you or didn't you? I'm not leaving until you answer."

His eyes narrowed. "And if I did?"

This was it. She'd bet he'd already hit a button somewhere alerting security. "Then you are an even bigger ass than I suspected. Because Lily deserves a father who'd go to the ends of the Earth to see her perform. And obviously you're not actually too busy for shit. You're just a sorry excuse for a daddy. I would know. I had one that would've moved Heaven and Earth to see me up on stage. But he died before getting that chance. And here you are. Alive and well. And how many shows of Lily's have you been to?"

"Miss Ryans, you will leave my office right this minute if you know what's good for you."

"How many?" she demanded.

"Miss Montgomery, I suggest you take your friend and—"

"How. Fucking. Many? Answer the question and I'll go."

His jaw ticked as he stood again. "You've made your point, now—"

"Just say it! Just admit that you haven't made it to a single show, that you haven't bothered to show your face a single solitary time to tell Lily she did a good job, or that you're proud of her and you love her. It's the truth, right?"

"Get out." Donovan Taite spoke through his teeth and livid hate burned from his eyes. Kylie took a deep breath. It was time to go. She could see that. But at least she'd tried.

"I'm going." Mia tugged her arm again, but Kylie jerked out of her reach. "Here." She slammed two tickets down on his desk. One was to the CMA festival in an hour and the other was for the Chameleon Café in Atlanta where their next show was. "I'll be expecting to see you at one or both of these, acting like Father of the Fucking Year. Bring flowers."

His eyes widened as Kylie glared at him.

"One more thing before I go. I've known Lily for a few months. You've known her for her whole life. Which one of us is acting like they actually give a shit about her right now?" When he didn't answer, she shook her head. And with that, she stormed out of his office in the same whirlwind fashion she'd blown into it.

"Holy hell," Mia said under her breath as they exited the reception area. "You might've just ended both of our careers, thank you very much."

"Yeah, you were a lot of help back there. 'Preciate it."

The elevator dinged and the two girls stepped on as soon as the doors were open. "Looked like you had it under control."

The temporary ceasefire on Mia's hatred of her ended later that afternoon. She sat on her bed, jotting down a few lyrics about what a wonderful man her father had been. She was trying to wrap a few of the sayings he was always reminding her of into a chorus when the door flew open so hard it nearly popped off the track.

She looked up from her notebook. Mia stood there, eyes blazing—red, as if she'd been crying. Her chest heaved and she clutched her phone in her hand. Kylie wondered if she should grab a pillow since Mia looked damn near ready to chuck it at her head.

"Mia?"

"He said my name today. Did you notice that?" Mia took a step inside the room.

She was practically vibrating with rage. *Jesus.* "Who said your name? I don't know what you're talking about."

"Donovan Taite. Donovan Taite knew my name even though you didn't give me two seconds to introduce myself. Care to know why that was?"

Kylie took a deep breath to calm the nerves Mia was riling up. "Um, because I told him who you were?"

"He knew before that. My agent just called. He was going to sign me. I was on his list of potential artists. He was planning to offer me a recording contract if everything went well on this tour. Guess who he just marked right off his list?"

Oh shit. Kylie blew out the breath she'd been holding. "Mia, I'm sorry. I didn't know. I never would've asked you to go with me if I'd—"

"If you'd what? Actually *thought* for a fucking minute before shooting your mouth off at the first person you felt like chewing out? Maybe you should start blowing up on that *perfect* boyfriend of yours instead of trashing other people's careers."

It wasn't like that. She'd been trying to do something for Lily. *No good deed goes unpunished.* She could add that to her list of things her daddy used to say. "Mia, I can call—"

"No. Do not do me any fucking favors. I mean it. Just leave me the hell alone." With that, Mia left, sliding the door shut behind her so hard it banged on the frame. Kylie flinched at the sound before dropping her head into her hands. She couldn't even call Trace to vent because he'd told her not to go there in the first place.

Why do I never listen?

CHAPTER Seventeen

He was late. Naturally. Because when it was time to leave, no one could find Gretchen. Why they couldn't just leave her ass in Louisville was beyond him. He should've been walking into the CMA Festival in downtown Nashville three hours ago when Kylie's show began. Instead, since Gretchen had decided to screw a bouncer in the bathroom of a bar, he was damn near sprinting through the crowd, sweating his ass off, and shoving people left and right. Danny, his fiddle player, had gone ahead of him.

Thankfully he'd been able to get a new phone as soon as they got into town. His very first text was from Kylie asking if she could borrow Danny and his banjo for one song. The old man had waggled his eyebrows at Trace, saying that pretty little thing could *borrow* him anytime she wanted. If it had been anyone else, Trace would've made him spit teeth. But Danny was the closest thing he had to a dad, and he knew he was just messing with him. He was pretty curious about the song Kylie needed him for though, and he damn sure wasn't going to miss it.

She'd forgiven him about the pictures once he'd proven to her they were promos. But things had still been strained between them. She'd sounded distant and cut calls short. He didn't like it. Missing the first show of hers he was supposed to be at probably wasn't going to help things any.

He needed to touch her, taste her, bury himself inside her until she remembered what they had and why it mattered.

When he got to the Vitamin Water stage where she was performing, he had to restrain himself to keep from climbing up onto it and wrapping her in his arms. It had been six long and shitty weeks without her. His dick had been keeping track of the minutes. It twitched at the sight of her.

"Hi y'all," her sweet voice drawled. "Usually the three of us close the show together but Lily had some…family issues to handle and Mia's helping her out. So I guess you're stuck with me tonight."

A few low whistles pierced the air as Trace made his way up front. Danny was up there with her, and she was sitting on a stool. He watched as she nodded at him to signal she was ready. Something was off. He could feel it, could see it. She usually looked like a damned superstar on stage, but tonight she seemed subdued. Sad even. His arms ached to wrap around her. *No.* They were keeping things as quiet as possible. Keeping the media out of it as much as they could manage. No need to taint his angel with his hellish reputation.

Danny strummed his banjo and Kylie's clear voice danced into the air. *"My daddy used to say, never let 'em see you sweat. Never let 'em see you cry. Girl you know better than that."*

Shit. The raw emotion in her voice broke over him. He didn't even know she'd been working on a song about her dad. Why didn't he know that? Oh yeah, because they hadn't seen each other in six damned weeks. For a moment he was back in Macon, watching the pain cross her face as she told him about her daddy. He shook his head and focused on his beautiful girl up on stage.

"My daddy used to say, never look down on a man. You look everyone in the eye, and you always shake hands." Danny strummed a bit and sped up the tempo. *"Cause you ain't no better and you ain't no worse. We all end up in the same ol' hearse."*

He watched as barely restrained ripples of hurt threatened

to roll across her face. Jesus. Watching her fight off her own pain stabbed him hard and deep in the chest.

"*He said there'd come a time to stand my ground, said there'd be a day when I didn't back down. Loved to remind me that what goes around always comes around. These are just the things my daddy used to say.*"

Danny stopped strumming altogether and Trace could see the moisture shining in her eyes. If he didn't know better, he'd think there was some in his too.

Deafening silence surrounded him in the seconds before she finished. Her voice was clear and strong when it pierced the air between them. "*When we laid him down in the cold hard ground, I knew it was time to walk away. But I'll never forget…the things my daddy used to say.*"

The second the applause hit, he was in motion. She was standing up there, forcing a smile for a bunch of strangers when she was dying inside. To hell with the media. He barely had time to register the look of surprise on her face when he jumped up on the stage and wrapped his arms around her. Her perfect mouth dropped open slightly so he covered it with his. And what began as a gesture of comfort soon turned to one of need. Desperate need. He didn't care who was watching or how many people had whipped out their damned cell phones to record it.

Kylie returned his kiss with the same heated ache that had been building up inside of him for six excruciating weeks. He felt her hands pull at his neck and he lifted her off the ground. When the cheers and whistles became painfully loud, he lowered her back down. She stepped back and grinned up at him through her thick, dark lashes. She was pink in the face, whether from the heat or the embarrassment of being mauled by her boyfriend on stage, he didn't know. Either way, she was the most beautiful sight he'd ever laid eyes on.

"I guess we're telling people now," she said softly, her breathy voice making him rock hard. They had to get the hell out of here. *Now.*

"Kylie Ryans, everybody!" he shouted into the mic as the

cheers continued. He grinned, the grin that usually earned him several pairs of panties being thrown on stage. But there was only one set of panties he was concerned about at the moment. He glanced over at his fiddle player, who was putting away the banjo he rarely used. "Danny, make sure everyone stays off the bus for…" He looked over at Kylie, who was wide-eyed and staring up at him. "At least an hour. No, shit, make it two." And with that, he picked his girlfriend up off her feet and carried her off stage.

CHAPTER Eighteen

"*Have* you lost your mind?" Kylie couldn't help but laugh at the crazy man practically running with her in his arms towards his bus.

"Yeah, I have." He licked his lips. "I think I left it with you because it's been missing since the last time I saw you."

"Trace Corbin, was that a line you just fed me?"

"Maybe. Did it work?" He raised a brow and glanced at her. The fierce determination in his eyes didn't waver even though Kylie was teasing him.

"Hmm. We'll see." She smirked, but inside she was a hot mess of want. She hadn't been ready for that song, but Lily was nearly hysterical when her dad didn't show, and Mia was still filled with rage and refusing to speak to her, much less close the show with her. It was the only thing Kylie could think to do. She knew Trace was coming and that his fiddle player also played the banjo. So she went for it. But when she'd taken the stage, she didn't see Trace anywhere. And the song about her daddy damn near killed her. Until he appeared out of nowhere and gave her exactly what she needed. Comfort. Affection. Was it love? Maybe. She didn't know for sure. She kind of hoped it was.

"I missed you, Kylie Lou," he said quietly. He placed a kiss on her forehead as he set her down just outside of his bus.

"I missed you, too," she told him. She took his hand, startled that his touch still sent her skin into a tingling frenzy. He did a quick scan of the bus and made sure it was empty. Kylie's stomach twisted both in nervousness at the thought of running into Gretchen Gibson, who she damn sure did not want to see—not right now anyways—and in anticipation of what she and Trace were about to do to each other. God. She'd missed him so much it was physically painful.

By the time they made it into Trace's room, she was practically trembling. She hoped he'd close the door, press her up against it, and show her just how much he'd missed her. He didn't. He closed the door and led her to the bed where they both sat. He reached out and tucked a stray hair behind her ear. She was slightly sweaty from performing out in the heat. She hoped she was about to get a whole lot sweatier.

"How have you been, Kylie Lou?" he asked, barely loud enough for her to hear. But she could hear what he wasn't saying. His eyes said he was just trying to be polite. That he really wanted to tear her clothes off and make the most of the two hours of alone time he'd secured for them. She was still raw and hurting from the tension she'd been living with for six weeks plus the pain of baring her soul and singing about her daddy. She wanted physical comfort. Wanted him inside of her. There'd be plenty of time for talking later.

"I've been…things are…there's been a lot going on and I do want to talk about it with you, but right now I just want…" How to phrase this particular request? She wasn't exactly sure.

"What do you want, pretty girl? Say the word and it's yours." Trace's eyes scanned her face for answers. Instead of speaking, she reached down and pulled her tank top over her head. His eyes widened but she wasn't stopping. She climbed onto his lap. Straddling him, she pulled his hat off and sat it next to them so she could run her fingers through his hair.

"That was my lucky hat," he mumbled against her lips.

"Oh, I think you're about to get plenty lucky without it." She deepened their kiss, pulling at his bottom lip with her teeth. She couldn't get enough of his tongue. His mouth was minty, as if he'd just brushed his teeth. For a split second she thought she tasted the faint hint of bourbon underneath. *Now isn't the time to grill him.* She lashed her tongue in and out of his mouth, pausing to run it over his teeth and lips. She felt his hardness beneath her so she ground her hips down against him.

Trace groaned and pulled her farther onto the bed. She'd never been on top before, but she was pretty damned excited about it.

She stood long enough to rid herself of her jeans. She was just about to climb back onto her boyfriend when he sat up abruptly.

"What are you doing?" she pouted.

"What are *you* doing?" He looked up at her, grinning as he grabbed her hips to pull her closer. "You think this is just going to be a quickie, then so long, see you in Atlanta tomorrow night?"

She smiled, remembering that he'd made sure their tours crossed paths a few times. Tomorrow after both of their shows in Georgia, they were spending the night at his house in Macon. She missed that place almost as much as she missed him.

"What are you grinning about, crazy girl?"

She winked. "Oh I have plans for tomorrow night."

He arched a brow. "What kind of plans?"

She cocked her head down towards him and whispered when she spoke. "Plans involving you finishing what you started in that shower. Plans involving me and you and that pond you dropped me into. Only, no clothes this time."

"My, haven't we been busy plotting."

"You have no idea." She couldn't take the sexy banter anymore so she lowered her head to place her mouth on his. His warm lips caressed hers perfectly. Kissing him was always like getting that exact thing she'd been craving. No disappointment or awkwardness—just pure pleasure. She loved kissing him, loved making love to him, loved writing music with him. Damn. She just flat out loved everything they did together. She was pretty sure this meant she loved *him*. Every time she thought about telling him, she remembered dancing with him at his birthday party. *I don't do relationships*, he'd said. But that was exactly what they were doing. Wasn't it?

Luckily, Trace was able to distract her from her concerns about unrequited love. She was still standing in her bra and panties. From his sitting position on the bed, he was at the perfect vantage point for placing his mouth on her. Which he did. Her head fell back as he looped a finger through her panties and pulled. Once they were down her legs, she kicked them to the side.

He licked her stomach and trailed his tongue to the top of her closely trimmed strip of hair. He pressed his mouth against her. "Damn, I've missed you," he growled against her tender flesh. Before she could respond, he grabbed her and pinned her down on the mattress. "Better," he mumbled as his mouth made its way down her throat, past her breasts, and over her stomach. His arms hooked her knees and pulled until she was spread open and exposed.

"Trace," she said barely loud enough to get his attention.

"Mmhm," he answered as his mouth continued traveling southbound.

"I want you so bad. It-it hurts." She throbbed so hard it was a struggle not to put her hand between her legs and press to relieve the pressure.

His head snapped up and his lust-filled gaze met hers. "I'm going to take care of you, baby. I promise."

She lifted her head over her black lacy bra-covered breasts and watched as he began placing gentle kisses on her. Surely he could feel how hard she was pulsating. It felt like that one spot was controlling her entire body. She squirmed, lifting her hips for more. Trace's breath tickled her and she whimpered.

"Please, Trace. *Please.*" She grabbed and tugged the comforter below her as tightly as she could.

"Please what, pretty girl?"

She groaned and lifted her hips once more.

"Say it, Kylie. Tell me what you want." His eyes were darker than usual. The way they got when he wanted a drink and she'd denied him. Now he was craving her and she wanted him to give in to that craving. Immediately.

"I want you to, t-to…make me come. Please."

"My pleasure, darlin'."

Oh hell. That was almost enough to send her into oblivion right there. She tensed as he finally placed one wet stroke of his tongue between her legs. She pulsed and ached for more. He licked her once more and she cried out. One more hard stroke of his tongue and she'd be gone. But he pulled back. "You want me here?" He trailed a finger through her slick folds before pressing it inside of her.

She couldn't answer so she nodded and her body convulsed beneath him.

He dipped his head but this time instead of a good hard lashing of his tongue, he swirled the tip around her clit. It was so intense she didn't know if what she felt was pleasure or pain.

"I-I want you. *Oh God.* Trace. I need you inside of me. *Now.*"

"First things first, darlin'." He pressed another finger slowly into her. Her body resisted the additional pressure. But then his tongue swiped her once more and she opened completely. The rush of him pressing so thick and full inside of her sent the room into a tailspin. He went in deep. Then he withdrew before going in more quickly this time. Before she realized what was happening, she was screaming. Actually screaming. His name. And a few obscenities she didn't make a habit of saying out loud. And the one word she'd probably always say when he wanted something from her. *Yes.*

She was still calling out in ecstasy when he eased on top of her and began removing his pants. She fumbled to help him. She was more than ready to have him inside of her.

"Trace." He didn't stop. Just yanked his shirt off and kicked his jeans onto the floor. *Good God a'mighty.* She was momentarily paralyzed by desire at the sight of him. Somehow she'd forgotten how muscular and perfect his body was. Her tongue danced behind her lips, aching to reach out and lick his smooth skin.

When his hard length sprang free from his boxer briefs, her

mouth watered. Actually watered. The juncture between her thighs heated, aching so intensely it felt as if her entire body was clenching.

Lauryn McCray popped into her head at that exact moment. Shit. She spoke in a frantic rush. "Um, Trace. I was thinking maybe we should use something. I haven't exactly been on a strict routine with my pill and with everything with—"

That stopped him cold. He looked as if she'd snapped him out of a trance, and she almost cried out in fear that she'd ruined the moment.

"It's not that I don't trust you. It's not about that at—"

"Shh, it's okay, baby. I've got something." He smiled and shook his head as he leaned to the left and opened the top drawer of the nightstand. She watched hungrily as he opened the foil packet and slid the latex over himself. He didn't sink into her right away like she'd expected. He dipped into her, just the head of him, and then pulled out and swirled her own slickness around her. *Sweet mother of orgasms.* Whoever said condoms didn't feel as good was doing it wrong.

She wrapped her legs around him and tried to pull him down onto her. Into her. He grinned and kissed her softly. "Didn't you want to be on top, pretty girl? I kind of got the impression that you did."

Even after six weeks apart he could still read her. She gave him a wicked grin and nodded. He grabbed her and rolled so that she was on top. The heady sense of control overtook her. *A girl could get used to this.*

He raised his arms, placing his hands behind his head and watching her with a dark interest. He cocked a brow as if to say *do your worst.*

Kylie's body warmed to a dangerous degree. *Challenge accepted.* She slid herself up his shaft, moaning at how good he felt against her sensitive flesh. When the tip of his erection met her opening, she used every ounce of self-control she had to lower herself onto him as slowly as humanly possible. Once he was all the way inside, her head fell back.

"Oh God, you're so *deep*." She rocked her hips slowly, not at all anxious to put any distance between him and that spot inside of her he was hitting perfectly. Her body turned to liquid as the soothing balm of pleasure spread through her.

"Lose the bra," Trace commanded. She did as she was told, fighting with the clasp before slinging it across the room. Once her breasts were bare, Trace began lifting his hips to meet her. His hands reached out and caressed her nipples. Gently at first and then rougher.

He'd had enough of her slow, steady rhythm. She could tell by the way his cock was expanding and jerking inside of her. He sat up, pulling her close so their bare chests pressed against each other. She began riding him faster as he clamped his mouth down on hers. His tongue massaged the inside of her mouth as his fingers kneaded into her backside. Trace's firm chest brushed against her soft breasts. That combination plus his dick stroking her G-spot had her ready to combust. The moans began slipping out without her permission.

Abruptly, he pulled back, gripping her tightly and forcing her eyes to meet his. "I've never wanted anything like I want you. Not a drink, not a drug, not even music. Not a single damned thing, Kylie. Do you understand that?"

She whimpered and nodded because it was the only way she could convey her understanding at the moment. And then everything exploded in a white hot flash. She was vaguely aware of the pinch of pain she felt as he bit down on one of her nipples. He began straining and groaning as he came beneath her. But her own release had her blind and mindless with a pleasure so intense it felt as if she were being torn from her body.

Panting, she collapsed on top of him. She trailed her fingertips around his chiseled chest as it rose and fell until she couldn't keep her eyes open any longer.

"Thank you," she mumbled softly. *For loving me*, she wanted to add but didn't. "For wanting me more than anything else," she said instead.

CHAPTER Nineteen

He'd told her once before. He didn't make love. And yet... what had just happened between them certainly wasn't fucking. Something had changed in him when he saw her up on that stage, giving the audience a part of her they didn't deserve. A part he hadn't even seen yet. He'd done what he'd done partly because he could see that she needed it. And partly because he'd been overcome with the need to possess her. To stake his claim on her. Because how long would it be before someone as amazing and strong and brave and talented as she was realized she could do better? How much time would it take for her to see that she was about to be a huge success and he wouldn't be worthy of working on her road crew? Though he would, happily, if she wanted him to.

How long until she realizes you've been drinking?

She was the most incredible woman he'd ever known. And she was only nineteen. She would probably be taking over the whole damned world by the time she was twenty-five. He watched as she slept. Her body barely moved as she inhaled and exhaled softly beside him. Watching her, being with her, just being *near* her, gave him a type of peace he'd never known. He was pretty sure this was what contentment felt like. She made him happy in a way nothing else ever could. It was true happiness, genuine and pure, not the kind you find at the bottom of a bottle. But if he'd learned anything, it was that these types of feelings were fleeting.

She'd said Gretchen was the female version of him and she'd been mostly right. Gretchen was making his life a living hell. Worse than hell. Hell would be a vacation resort in the Caribbean compared to touring with Gretchen. Knowing he'd been the same brand of selfish and toxic when Kylie had joined him on his last tour made him want to kick his own ass. She deserved so much better than that. She deserved someone who could give her forever. A future. Promises that would be kept. All he could give her was today. Today he was sober. Yesterday he hadn't been. Tomorrow he couldn't speak for. But for the first time in his entire life, he wanted to make promises. More than that, he wanted to be able to actually keep them.

A thick knot formed in his throat, constricting his airways. She was smiling a little in her sleep. Her face was smooth, not at all like the tense expression she'd had on stage earlier. She could fake the audience out all day long, but she'd never be able to fake it with him. Damn that made him happy, like cat-ate-the-damn-canary happy. He was so proud of her. Proud of her strength, of her talent, and of how beautiful she truly was inside and out.

He lightly stroked the side of her face, grinning as she wrinkled her cute little nose at his touch. His stomach clenched as she shivered and then resumed her content little smile. Was this what falling in love felt like? He wondered if he was falling in love with her right that minute. Hell, maybe he already had and his stupid ass was just now catching up.

He forced his throat to swallow as he brushed a strand of hair from her face. He'd enjoy their time together while he could. Savor it like the bittersweet burn of the last drop of bourbon. Because he knew it'd be hell letting her go. But some day, when she realized that he'd just hold her back, he'd have to. That was very likely going to be the same day he'd lose his already faltering grip on sobriety completely. He was pretty sure that knowing that wouldn't give him any kind of advantage over it. Just like knowing he wasn't good enough for Kylie Ryans wouldn't make it any easier to let her go.

"*Shit!*" A loud banging sound startled him awake. Trace rolled his neck and sat up in bed. Kylie was still sleeping soundly next to him. Glancing over at the alarm clock on the night table, he saw it was just after midnight. Oh hell, her bus was probably already on the way to Atlanta by now. Not that it was a big deal. They were headed there as well. He just figured he should've asked her if she wanted to ride with him instead of screwing her into a coma and kidnapping her. Mia and that other chick touring with her were probably good and pissed.

He heard more swearing from Gretchen as she stumbled to her room. The room that used to be Kylie's. Damn, he missed those days. Well, kind of. His dick didn't miss the long nights of knowing she was just a few feet away. Especially once she'd started making it painfully clear that she wanted him as badly as he wanted her. If that was even possible.

"Kylie Lou," he said softly, rubbing her arm just firmly enough to wake her. "Babe, you might want to call Mia or your manager or both and let them know you're catching a ride to Atlanta with me."

He watched as she opened her beautiful blue eyes and blinked several times. "Mmm. So it wasn't a dream then." She grinned and he cocked a brow at her.

"A dream?"

She bit her lip in that way that made him want to do the same. "I thought I dreamed you. I've been dreaming of you a lot lately."

He leaned down to kiss her firmly on the mouth. Because he had to. Brushing his nose against hers, he smiled. "As much as I want to hear about these dreams of yours in explicit detail, you really need to call and let the girls know where you are."

The clouded haze of sleep cleared and she sat straight up, nearly slamming her head against his as she did. "Oh no. Crap. I don't have my phone."

"Here," he said, handing her his new one from its place on the nightstand.

She stared at it. "Um, I don't actually know their numbers."

Trace cleared his throat. Well, this was about to get awkward. "Mia's is in there," he said, hoping she wouldn't read more into this than necessary. They'd transferred his old numbers to his new phone. He kind of wished they hadn't.

"Okay." She didn't look mad, but she was suddenly very interested in scrolling through his contacts to get to Mia's name. That was a bad thing for more reasons than his still sex-fogged brain could count.

Her jaw clenched as she avoided his gaze. She continued avoiding him as she called Mia and told her in a clipped tone that she was sorry and would see them in Atlanta.

"Hey." He reached out a finger and tilted her chin so she had to look him in the eye. What he saw in hers stole his breath. Hurt. Fear. Most likely a fear of being hurt. "Don't look like that. I don't delete shit from my phone because I'm too lazy to fool with it."

"Lots of numbers in there," she said softly, handing his phone back. He heard what she didn't say. Lots of *women's* numbers in there.

"Kylie." He shifted into her line of vision as she tried to look away. Once her gaze was firmly locked on his, he continued. "You could throw that phone right out the window and I swear to God I wouldn't blink. There isn't a number in there I give a damn about more than you. And I know your number by heart." He watched her eyes darken, knowing she was deciding whether or not to trust him.

"Oh my God, do you have a girl in there?" Gretchen shrieked before Kylie had a chance to say anything. "Jesus, Corbin. Feel free to bring your whores on the bus. Guess I can bring whoever I want on here too from now on."

"Go sleep it off, Gretchen," he hollered back.

His girlfriend gaped at him in horror. *Welcome to my life.*

CHAPTER Twenty

Kylie pulled the sheet up to cover her naked body. Trace's expression was annoyed, but he didn't seem concerned that Gretchen was about to barge in on them or anything. She relaxed a little, but still grabbed his shirt and buttoned it over herself.

"Do you have any idea what seeing you in my shirt does to me?"

She smirked at him after she'd finished with the last button. "Brings back fond memories of me kicking your ass in that mud fight?"

He snorted. "Something like that. What do I have to do to get a rematch?" He leaned in to kiss her but she stiffened. The press of his lips softened her, but just barely. Gretchen's very presence on the bus with them made her tense. The pictures she'd seen of the woman pawing her boyfriend were promo shots. She got that. She knew it was true. But it didn't take away the wounds from the sharp, stabbing knife of betrayal that had carved through her when she saw them the first time. The website had plastered them on its home page with headlines screaming that he and Gretchen Gibson were an item, that they were out on the town, and that he didn't give two shits about his little fling with what's-her-face.

Just knowing someone had the power to hurt her like that twisted her up inside. Made her wonder why in the world she thought she could hold on to a man who had women like Gretchen around. Women who'd get drunk and have a good time with him instead of pouring out his entire liquor cabinet. Women who knew their way around a bedroom and probably a few other places. One thing she knew for sure. It was important to size up your competition.

"I want to meet her," she informed Trace as she stood up to pull her jeans back on.

He looked at her as if she'd just told him she wanted to give up music and take up space exploration. "You want to what?"

She rolled her eyes. Pulling her just-fucked hair into a ponytail, she turned and got in one last look at his naked body. "Get dressed. I want you to introduce me."

"That is literally the worst idea you've ever had. No."

She frowned. "Yeah, I wasn't asking. Either you can introduce me or I can walk out there and introduce myself." She reached for the handle on his door.

He muttered something unintelligible under his breath. "Give me a sec."

She admired his back muscles as they strained against each other while he got dressed. For a moment she considered saying to hell with meeting Gretchen Gibson and just crawling right back into bed with him. But they were still a few hours away from Atlanta. There'd be time for that.

Trace stood and took her hand, which she appreciated. She gave it a gentle squeeze. No matter what she'd said, she had a feeling he knew Gretchen still bothered her. Well, not Gretchen herself exactly. Just the *idea* of her.

They stepped out into the common area of the bus but the woman was nowhere to be seen.

"Gretch," Trace called out. Oh for the love. That hurt to hear. Not that he said it with any kind of emotion behind it or anything, but just the fact that he'd called the woman by anything other than her complete name stung a bit.

"What?" a harsh voice called back from the direction of the room where Kylie had slept when she was on tour with him. *Salt in the wound.* Lots of it. The kind from the giant container with the pour spout and the chick with the umbrella on it.

"Can you come out here a sec?" Trace sounded exactly as excited about this little impromptu meeting as he looked. Which was not at all.

When the woman appeared, in nothing but an oversized black Lynyrd Skynyrd T-shirt no less, Kylie sucked in a breath. Gretchen Gibson was all curves and long, thick ink-black hair swinging down her back. She had that rough look about her, like she'd been rode hard and put up wet, her daddy used to say. She looked like she could probably hogtie a steer in the time it took Kylie to put on lip gloss. But she was beautiful at the same time. Her bright, crystal clear gray eyes against her dark features made her striking, and her swagger made it clear she knew she was gorgeous. *Well that's not intimidating at all.*

"Gretchen Gibson, this is Kylie Ryans. She wanted to meet you," Trace said with no emotion in his voice. She didn't miss that he didn't call her his girlfriend. But he still held her hand, so she took that as a good sign.

"Pleasure to meet you," Kylie said, sticking out the hand Trace wasn't holding. The other woman eyed it with disinterest all over her face. Kylie dropped her hand and ran it through her hair. "My daddy was a big fan of yours."

Gretchen raised an eyebrow. "Oh yeah? Was? He's not anymore?"

Kylie swallowed hard. It was time to stop breaking apart inside every time this came up. "He passed away last year. Right before Christmas."

"Sorry to hear that." But the woman didn't look sorry. She didn't look…anything. Except maybe bored with the entire hassle of existing. As if being alive was somehow putting her out.

Kylie shrugged. "Anyways, I just wanted to meet you. Wanted to wish you luck on the tour." She forced a smile. Which Gretchen didn't return.

The woman sneered and glanced up at Trace. "S̶ More like you wanted to see if I was planning to fuck your m̶ Am I right?"

Trace stepped between them. "That's enough. Don't be a bitch, Gretchen. Or are you even able to switch that off?"

Kylie appreciated his gesture, but she could take care of herself. She was from the trashy side of town. She'd dealt with the worst of them in high school. Gretchen was obviously the damaged, pretend-I-don't-give-a-shit-and-lash-out-at-you-first variety of female. "It's okay. I saw all I needed to. Pleasure meeting you, Ms. Gibson." Kylie smiled as widely as possible. If anything was going on, she'd bet her ass Gretchen would've been sweet as Grandma's apple pie to her. But the woman was obviously pissed off and annoyed by her presence. Likely because Trace *wasn't* paying her the attention she wanted. *Thank God.*

She pulled at Trace's hand, ready to go back in the bedroom and enjoy their last few hours together, but Gretchen's feathers were ruffled. "What the hell is that supposed to mean?"

Again, Trace stepped closer, putting a hand up to stop Gretchen from advancing on them. "It means she wanted to meet you and she did. So goodnight."

Kylie scoffed out loud. Surely he knew she wasn't going to let him start speaking for her, regardless of what they did to each other behind closed doors. "No, actually I meant you're nothing like I thought you'd be and I doubt Trace would even be interested in you. Obviously the tabloids got it wrong. So I can sleep easy from now on."

"Well, *actually*, Trace was plenty inter—"

"Shut the hell up, Gretchen. Or I swear to God, I'll call Noel Davies right this second and call this whole thing off. This isn't just my last chance, sweetheart. It's yours too." The acid in Trace's voice kept Kylie from caring that he'd called Gretchen sweetheart. He very clearly meant it in the meanest way possible. But what the hell had Gretchen been about to say?

"You know what? I'm going to bed. Kylie, you might want to

check with the driver to see if there's a car seat on the bus you could use."

Wow, that was original. This woman wasn't nearly as sharp as she looked. And screw her for not knowing the driver's name. Kylie liked him. Missed him. Juanita, the woman driving her bus, barely even spoke to anyone. "Thanks for your concern. While I'm at it, I'll see if *Carl* can locate your dignity. Or that last ounce of class you must've dropped on your way in. Lovely perfume you're wearing, by the way." Kylie inhaled. "Smells like drunken bartender and piss-drenched back alley. Bet your evening was super special."

Gretchen launched herself towards her, but she didn't flinch. Trace braced his arms around Gretchen before she reached her and walked her backwards.

"Night night, *Gretch*," Kylie called out from over his shoulder.

After Trace had practically shoved Gretchen into her room, he returned to Kylie. She was a smidge embarrassed about her behavior, but at the same time, she was who she was. He knew that. He could take it or leave it. But she hoped he wouldn't leave it. So she hopped up on the counter in the kitchenette and leaned back to watch him approach.

Once he was situated between her legs, in the same position he'd been in once before in that very same spot, he quirked a brow. "Was that fun for you?"

She narrowed her eyes. "No. I didn't know she was going to be so hateful to me. But I give what I get. You know that. Why? Was it fun for you?"

He pressed himself tighter in between her legs. She shivered as his breath tickled her jawline. "Mm, maybe. A little. I like seeing you all worked up. But I like it better when you work all that aggression out on me."

"Me too." She grinned up at him from under her lashes.

He made a low growling sound in her ear. "Let's go back to my room."

Yes, please. "Wait." She put a hand on his chest and looked into his hooded hazel eyes. "Tell me something."

"Anything, as long as you promise we can go back to bed." He brushed his face against hers. Damn, she loved how his stubbled jaw felt on her smooth skin.

"Why'd you stop? That night, here, when we were—" She interrupted herself to wave a hand between them.

Trace exhaled loudly. He leaned back and ran a hand through his hair. "Jesus, Kylie. We barely knew each other and I was…and you were…" He shook his head.

"Well, that clears that up."

He grunted. "You know what I mean. I told you that night. You deserved better." He leaned closer, letting her pull him in with her legs, which she'd wrapped around his waist when he started to step back. "You still do."

She rolled her eyes. There was no one better for her as far as she was concerned. She lifted her hips to get him against her like she needed. "And yet, you're not stopping this time."

Trace smiled, his one-of-a-kind panty-dropping smile as he pressed against her. "I'm *trying* to be better."

She couldn't help but smile back. "How's that working for you?"

"You tell me, Kylie Lou," he said just before he placed his lips gently against hers. She whimpered when he sucked her bottom lip into his mouth.

"I think you're pretty damn good just the way you are."

She wrapped her arms tightly around his neck, losing herself in his kiss completely as he carried her back to his room.

CHAPTER Twenty One

The sexy breathy little moans his girlfriend let out threatened to end him every time. Those noises haunted his dreams when they were apart. He sank into her slick tightness, groaning as he did. She was made for him. That was the only explanation he could come up with.

"Trace," she pleaded in a deep husky tone that killed him a little bit. "I want it harder this time."

Christ. He rammed into her, roughly jolting her body in a way that made him want to growl like a crazed animal, letting everyone in the tri-state area know she was his and his alone, dammit. He bit down on her mouth as they kissed. She whimpered again, so he raked his teeth against her bottom lip hard enough to hurt. She was channeling her frustration from that night months ago when he'd left her hanging on the countertop. He'd bet his farm on it.

But he wasn't ready for it to be over, not by a long shot. Not when he had one more day before they went back to living separate lives. Lives where he couldn't see her smiling face, kiss her smart, sassy mouth, and bury himself inside of her. So he pulled as far out of her as he could, staring straight down into her eyes as he went. When he sank back into her, she closed her eyes and arched her back. His gaze trailed down the smooth column of her throat. His mouth licked, kissed, and sucked every inch of skin within his reach.

"Tell me something," he rasped into her ear.

"Anything." The whisper of her voice combined with the inferno raging around his dick was almost too much. He pressed as deeply into her as he could go.

"Before…when we were—*oh fuck*." He bit off another swear word as her walls clenched around him.

"You were saying?" she asked sweetly. She kissed his neck this time, and he was surprised how much he enjoyed it. No one had ever kissed him there before. At least, not when he was sober enough to remember it.

"When was the first time, the first time you realized you would be with me if I wanted?" It was a cocky prick of a question to ask but he'd been going insane reminiscing about their all too brief time together. Wondering why she would've fallen for him when he was such a mess.

She clenched around him again. And again. He pressed harder, the tip of his dick hitting farther than it ever had in an attempt to hold her still. But her walls were full on pulsating around him now. "Jesus. Is that you doing that? I mean, on purpose?"

She grinned, an impish little smirk that said yes she damn sure was doing that on purpose.

"You keep that up and I'm going to come before you do." He used every ounce of strength he had to pull himself out of her clenching depths. "Answer the question, please."

She let out a throaty noise of disapproval. "I'm not sure I understand what you're asking exactly." She was panting slightly and her hot breath on him was almost more than he could take.

"When would you have fucked me, Kylie Lou? At what point would you have let me pick you up, press you against the wall, and make you scream my name?" He forced his dick back into her throbbing walls, sinking heavily into her welcoming heat.

She pulsed faster and he couldn't hold out any longer. He

resumed moving inside of her, matching the intense rhythm her body set for them. Sweet noises escaped her throat, pleasure and pain and need mingling together in the space between them.

"Tell me." He thrust hard into her, once, twice. Her back bowed, forcing her bare breasts into his chest. He reached a hand up to cup one. Leaning down he pulled each of her sweet, tight nipples into his mouth. "Tell me when," he demanded against her breast.

She didn't answer, but judging from her moans, she was close. Despite his own intense need, he withdrew until she cried out. "Please, Trace. *Please don't stop.*"

"I won't. I promise. Just tell me when, pretty girl."

Her panting became frantic. He looked down into her eyes. They were wide, like a frightened animal's. Desperate. "That first night," she whispered.

"On the bus?" Well that was a surprise. He'd been a complete asshole because she'd intimidated the hell out of him on stage. He rammed hard into her, filling her completely and then pulling out once more.

She shook her head as she writhed beneath him. "No. In the Rum Room. After we sang." Her words blurred together as she rushed them out of her mouth. She closed her eyes but he needed them open. This was one hell of a shock to his system.

"Look at me. The first night we met, when you didn't know me from Adam?"

She opened her eyes and nodded before closing them again. Pain stabbed him down low in his stomach. Was this all about who she thought he was? *What* he was instead of *who* he really was? He'd thought it was so much more than that. He didn't think he was wrong. "Why?"

He watched as she swallowed hard and opened her beautiful blues. He slid in and rocked gently inside of her, drowning in her gaze as she licked her lips. "I was broken. Dead inside," she whispered. "You made me feel alive."

That was it. The last nudge he needed to jump off the cliff into the abyss that was loving Kylie Ryans. She pulsed once more around him and he released himself inside of her with everything he had.

"Everything will be different now," she said softly into the darkness.

"Hmm?" Trace was drifting into that murky area between sleep and consciousness.

"Everyone knows. That we're together. Or they will soon."

"That okay?" The concern in Kylie's voice dragged him back to the surface. He pulled her closer and met her sleepy stare.

She nodded, wiggling closer to him. "Just…I don't want to do anything that's going to mess things up for you. I tend to feel first and think second. I don't know if you've noticed…" She smiled and he couldn't resist kissing her luscious mouth. God, she always tasted so damn good. Sweet and savory, like vanilla and honey.

"Babe, I'm the one who'd mess things up for you. I wanted to keep us quiet so people wouldn't make any judgments about you based on my sorry ass. You're new to this business and you deserve to make a name for yourself without mine tainting that."

She snorted. "I've never been one to care what people think, Trace."

"I know. Believe me, I love that about you. But this business is…"

"Is what?" she asked, tilting her chin up at him.

"Is all about what people think. Whether they like you, your sound, your latest single, your album, your look, your—"

She cut him off with a deep kiss. When she was done, she brushed her nose against his. "I'm with you, Trace. My music is my music. I give it everything I have. If people don't like me, either because of you or because of my music, well…they can change the damn channel. Or station. Or whatever."

He smiled. She was so much smarter and so much stronger than him. He'd let it all get to him. Made it personal. All of it. The media, the label, the shitstorm that came whenever he didn't follow protocol. He'd floundered around like a fish out of water as he tried to make a name for himself while figuring out who he was. The woman in his arms knew who she was already. He was pretty sure she knew who he was too. And yet…she was still here.

"I shouldn't have ambushed you like that tonight," he mumbled against her lips.

"I didn't mind." Kylie nuzzled down into the area between his shoulder and his neck, kissing his chest lightly as she did. Her head fit perfectly. Again, he was struck by the overwhelming knowledge that she was made for him. He closed his eyes when the room threatened to spin. He wanted a drink. And he wanted to kick his own ass for wanting it.

"Why'd you sing that song, Kylie Lou? The one about your dad? I mean, don't get me wrong, it was…it was amazing. Different for you, but amazing. But it looked…painful."

She sighed and he gave her a little squeeze. "Mia pretty much hates me and Lily was dealing with a situation with her dad. We usually close the shows together. But Lily's dad didn't show, *again*, and she was hysterical. I'd already used all my material." He felt her shrug against him. "It was that or the Cup Song. And I didn't have a cup."

He grinned. "Well it's a good song. A great song. I just couldn't watch you up there, hurting like you were, and not do something about it." He kissed her on top of the head but she was stiff in his arms.

When she spoke her voice was barely more than a whisper. "Funny, that's exactly how I felt about you when we were on tour together."

Chapter Twenty Two

After her show in Atlanta, Kylie was jittery with anticipation. Trace had his own show across town so he couldn't make hers. But he was meeting her later at a restaurant downtown called The Tavern. Technically, it would be their first date.

Trace's sister Rae and her friends had come to see her show and had hung out backstage while she got ready. Rae insisted she wear a dress. Kylie twirled in the full-length mirror, smiling to herself as the red fabric swung loosely just below her thighs.

"You should wear heels," Rae informed her. Both of her friends nodded in agreement.

"As much as I want to break an ankle and end up in the ER at the end of the night, I'm gonna pass on that suggestion."

Rae frowned. "But they elongate your legs."

Kylie rolled her eyes as she slipped into her favorite pair of boots. "You've been reading too many fashion magazines, Rae."

She was just about to tell the girls they could stay as long as they liked and hang out with Lily when a loud knock sounded on the dressing room door. "Come in," she called out.

Her mouth nearly popped open when the door did. Lily was

tucked under the arm of a familiar man in a suit. Kylie's eyes widened. She was holding a bouquet of lilies.

"Ms. Ryans, it's a pleasure to see you again." Donovan Taite cleared his throat and reached out a hand. "You look lovely when you're not instilling fear into the hearts of hardened businessmen, by the way."

She couldn't help but grin as she shook his hand. "Mr. Taite, how nice of you to grace us with your presence. I take it you caught the show?"

The broad man nodded and glanced at Lily with what Kylie believed was pride. "Well I certainly couldn't miss it after you so thoughtfully hand delivered my ticket, now could I? Pretty impressive. All three of you actually. I think you might have something with that bit there at the end."

She was starting to think so herself. The song they'd written together seemed to be a hit in the making. Mia still hated her guts, but so far she hadn't stabbed her to death in her sleep. That was something at least.

"Well, I have a…um, prior engagement, but I'm glad you came." It was the truth. Lily was lit up like a thousand-watt light bulb.

Kylie hugged Rae and told her she'd see her later before saying goodbye to Lily. Just as she pulled the door open to leave, Donovan Taite cleared his throat. "Ms. Ryans?"

She turned and cocked her head in his direction.

"I'm not a perfect man. I make mistakes. When I'm wrong, I say so." She raised an eyebrow, trying to picture the look on Trace's face when she told him she'd gotten a sort of apology out of *The* Donovan Taite. "Thank you for coming to see me. For…saying some things I needed to hear."

She took a deep breath. "You're welcome. It was my pleasure." She winked at him and shot a quick grin at Lily. *See? Being a hothead wasn't the worst thing in the world.* She'd have to be sure and tell Trace that. In a half hour when she saw him. Excitement danced inside of her, electrifying every nerve ending in her body. Last night had been nice, but it had included Gretchen. Tonight would just be about them. She also hoped this meant she hadn't blown Mia's shot of getting signed with BackRoom Records after all.

"I hope it's all right to say so, but I think if your daddy had been here to see you tonight, he'd have been proud."

Unexpected tears welled up in her eyes. "Um, thank you, sir. That's nice to hear."

Kylie left the Chameleon Café, where they'd just brought down the house, feeling as if she were walking on air. For the first time since she'd started chasing this dream, it was starting to feel like she might have actually caught it. And low and behold, miracle of all miracles, she had someone to share it with.

She took a cab to The Tavern after promising Lily and Mia she'd be back on the bus on time tomorrow afternoon. Lily had told her to have a good time. Mia had given her the usual death glare. Trace had invited all three girls to stay at his house but they'd gotten a hotel. Kylie smirked to herself as she thought about why. She was actually pretty excited about being alone with him. Well, aside from his sister Claire Ann and possibly Rae if she was staying at the farm this weekend. But their rooms were at the opposite end of the house. *God bless whatever builder designed the floor plan.*

The Tavern was a cute little place tucked into a quaint street lined by trees and streetlamps. An expensive-looking boutique and an ice cream shop bordered it. White twinkle lights lit the trees. It was like walking into a dream. But this was real. Trace Corbin was taking her on a date. She was grinning like a maniac as she stepped inside and told the maître d' she was waiting for someone.

"Ah yes, Ms. Ryans? We've been expecting you."

She took the man's arm because he offered it. He escorted her past the main dining area and towards the kitchen. Tucked into a corner she never would have noticed was a small table. Candlelight reflected on Trace's clean-shaven face. He'd been stubbly yesterday. Her stomach tensed. He'd shaved for her. Tonight they weren't Kylie Ryans, up and comer, or Trace Corbin, troubled superstar.

They were just two people enjoying an evening together. Just as her escort released her, Trace stood. Hot damn, he cleaned up good. Her mouth went dry. She licked her lips as she approached the table.

He wore dark jeans—nice ones like he wore for his shows, not the tattered ones he usually wore when they were just hanging out. His black dress shirt was rolled up at the sleeves. Her breath caught when their eyes met. He smiled his warm *I adore you* smile, and her legs began moving of their own accord. It felt like… like she was walking towards more than just her boyfriend. In that moment, Kylie felt like she was walking towards the one thing she needed more than air. *Home.*

"Hey, pretty girl," he said, giving her an appreciative once-over. "You trying to kill me with that dress?"

"You look pretty handsome yourself." Jesus. She suddenly felt shy. Which was nuts. This wasn't some guy she barely knew. They'd seen each other naked. Less than twenty-four hours ago. And yet… she was so nervous her whole body was shaking. Trace leaned in and kissed her cheek. He smelled like warmth and expensive cologne. And…something else. *If he's drinking again, he'd tell me. Wouldn't he?*

He pulled out her chair and she sat, watching his every move as he made his way to his own seat. "I hope this is okay. This is the most private table they have."

"It's perfect." She tried to breathe normally and ignore the strange feeling in her stomach.

Trace grinned, revealing the boyish dimples that framed his perfect mouth. "They have the best steak here. Seriously. You better order one for yourself because you're not getting any of mine."

At that, she laughed and her nerves eased up a bit. "Oh, I bet you'd give me a bite if I asked nicely."

He eyed her from over the top of his menu. "Do you ask for things nicely? I don't think I've ever seen you do that before."

With her stomach clenching from the heat in his stare, Kylie put her menu aside. "Maybe you've never had anything I wanted badly enough to ask nicely for."

He raised a brow and opened his mouth to respond. But at that same moment, a waitress appeared and asked for their drink order. Kylie didn't miss how flustered the girl became when she got an eyeful of Trace. It would've been irritating, but really, with the way he looked tonight, Kylie couldn't blame her. She was still trying to get a handle on her own self.

When the waitress left, Trace leaned across the table. "Actually, I take that back. I've heard you ask nicely a time or two. Matter of fact, it bordered on begging. I think it went something like, 'Oh God, yes, *please*. Trace, *please*.'"

Heat crawled over her skin at his imitation of her. Barely keeping the grin of embarrassment from her face, she shook her head. "You're not right. What kind of thing is that to say to a girl on a first date?"

He grinned back, the promise of something dark gleaming in his eyes. "Considering this date is going to end with that dress on my bedroom floor and your legs wrapped around my neck, I think it's a perfectly acceptable thing to say."

Good Lord. What was she going to do with this man? Oh yeah. Exactly what he'd just described. "Not if you don't buy me dessert it isn't. No dessert, no love."

Trace leaned back in his seat, easing up the intensity of his stare and allowing her to finally breathe normally. "Hmm, I'll think about it."

A half hour later, they were discussing how their shows had gone and enjoying their steaks. So naturally, she had to go and ruin it.

She cleared her throat. This conversation had been put on hold long enough and it was time, whether she liked it or not. "So, any chance you're going to tell me how this ended up being a co-headlining tour?"

Trace sighed and put his fork down. Propping his elbows on the table, he leaned forward.

"Yeah. But in the interest of full disclosure, I probably have to go back further than that."

Kylie put her own fork down and took a sip of her sweet tea. "Okay."

Trace took a deep breath before he began. "I've been wanting this type of tour for as long as I've been with Capital. Outdoor venues, cheaper tickets, tailgating style, you know? I'm nothin' special. Just a regular guy. I wanted anyone who wanted to hear my music to be able to come and just have a good time. Let loose, drink a few beers, and enjoy a decent show." He shrugged and Kylie fought the urge to correct him. She'd seen him perform. He put on so much more than a *decent show.* But his eyes were getting that far away look and she knew it was best to let him talk while he was in the mood to open up.

"The label seemed to be going for it. Finally. Honestly, I probably have you to thank for that. The rumors about us, the Cinderella story stuff, made me look like Prince Charming instead of Captain Panty Dropper as you so lovingly refer to me."

He winked and she laughed out loud.

"Anyways, as soon as the venues are all set and everything's falling into place, Noel Davies drops this bomb on me. On all of us really. Gretchen is my co-headliner, and it's either suck it up and deal or Bryce Parker can take my place. On *my* tour. The one I've been working my ass off to arrange."

Kylie winced. "Ouch." *Maybe I don't want to sign with his label after all.*

"Yeah." Trace huffed out a breath and then took a drink of his Coke. "That's not the worst part."

She held her breath, unsure as to what to expect.

"I knew Gretchen…before. And Noel Davies knows that."

The air whooshed from her lungs. There was something about the way he said *knew* that hit her wrong. "Knew as in…"

For a split second he looked as if he were in pain, but then he continued. "As in when I first moved to Nashville with a few guys I was in a band with, she sort of joined up with us. Her real name is Gretchen Warner, and she's from a small coastal town in South Carolina. But she had a Gibson Hummingbird, similar to yours actually. She was in love with it. I mean, in love. As in I think she slept with it in her bed. So another guy in the band started calling her Gibson. And Gretchen Gibson was born." Trace shook his head. Kylie tried to ignore the ache caused by his tone. He held some type of affection for Gretchen in his voice. It was subtle, but she could hear it.

"Anyways, we were all young and stupid. No offense." He winked and she rolled her eyes.

"None taken."

"A bunch of shit happened and the band broke up. Not exactly on amicable terms either. She went off and did her own thing and so did the rest of us. We…crossed paths a few times but that was that. Guess who her very first agent was?"

Kylie backtracked through her mind and tried to put the pieces together. "Noel Davies?"

"Name your prize, pretty lady."

Kylie smirked. "Okay, but I still don't get it? Why force her off on you?"

She watched as his forehead wrinkled over his brow. He rubbed his neck for a moment before meeting her gaze. "She's a mess. You were dead on when you called her the female version of me. She drinks like a pirate, pisses herself on stage, flashes the audience if she gets it in her screwed up head to do so. I think the only reason people even buy tickets to her concerts is so they can say they saw whatever outrageous shit she does next. Davies can't say to hell with her because she probably knows more about him than anyone. So he added a *conduct unbecoming* clause to the contract for this tour. If either of us screws up and breaches the contract, he's free of us courtesy of the label's new policy. Like me, Gretchen's all out of favors. So what better way to cut two fuck-ups loose than to stick them together? We're gasoline and matches, and all Capital has to do is sit back and wait for the explosion."

If she disliked Gretchen Gibson before, she downright hated her now. "Trace, you can't let them do this. It isn't fair. It's not… right."

He shrugged and picked up his knife and fork. "It is what it is. I had my chance. I had several chances. I screwed up and now I have to take what I can get. Even if it's…well, you know."

She watched as he finished off the last bite of his steak. "But you're doing better. You're working so hard and—"

"Lots of people work hard, Kylie Lou. Doesn't mean we always get what we want. Besides, Gretchen isn't out to get me or anything. She's too busy ruining her own life to interfere with mine all that much."

She handed the waitress her plate and bit her lip as he did the same. It sure as hell felt like Gretchen was interfering on their night right now so she changed the subject. "Oh," she said as the waitress sat her Tiramisu in front of her. "I never got the chance to tell you that I went to see Donovan Taite."

Trace had just taken a bite of his cheesecake. He swallowed and then gaped at her. "No shit?"

She nodded. "No shit. And um, it didn't go all that well."

"Kylie, I told you not to—"

"He came to the show tonight, Trace. And get this, he told me I was right and he was wrong and he thanked me. Sort of. And he said my daddy would be proud if he could see me." She placed a spoonful of her dessert in her mouth and her eyes closed involuntarily. Damn, it was good. She'd have settled for ice cream at the little shop she'd seen on her way in. But even a scoop of mint chocolate chip couldn't compare to this.

When she opened her eyes, Trace was watching her. She couldn't decipher what was going on in his gaze, which was unusual. She'd gotten pretty good at reading him. "What?"

He shook himself out of his trance. "Nothing. Just thinking that I am majorly screwed. If you can bring a man like Donovan Taite to his knees, then I don't stand a chance."

A grin broke out over her face. "Hmm, you on your knees. Now where have I seen than before?"

Trace's eyes widened and he nearly choked on his cheesecake.

"Ah yes, the shower date you owe me."

"You finished?" he asked, jerking his head towards her plate.

"I am now." She stared into his scorching gaze. God, she loved those eyes.

He didn't break eye contact for a single second as his arm shot into the air. "Check, please."

Chapter Twenty Three

"Close your eyes," Trace told her as they walked out into the warm Georgia night.

"What? Why?" His girlfriend shot him an annoyed look and he couldn't help but smirk back at her.

"Just do it. Please, for me?" He put his arm around her so he could guide her in the direction he wanted. "See? I can ask nicely, too."

She shook her head but did as she was told. He walked her around to the place where he'd parked her surprise.

"Okay, open."

She didn't say anything, but her mouth dropped open into that little O of surprise he loved. When she turned to him, her eyes said more than her mouth ever could. She was shocked, sad, happy, and grateful. He couldn't hold back anymore, so he did what he'd been wanting to do since she'd strutted up in the restaurant in that damn dress. His lips sought hers out as she clung to him. Her tongue pressed into his mouth, and he tasted the sweet cream and espresso flavor of her dessert. Once they were both out of breath, he pulled back. "So you like it then?"

She nodded, glancing back at the red and gray '88 Chevy pickup in the parking lot. "I love it. Is it—"

"It is," he confirmed her unfinished question as he led her to the driver's side. "And Lord help me, I'm going to let you drive us to the house."

She grinned and leaned up for another kiss. "How'd you get it? Oh God, Trace. Please tell me you didn't steal it."

He laughed as he helped her up into the cab. He jogged around to the passenger side and hopped in. "No, Kylie Lou, I didn't steal it. I negotiated. I can be very persuasive when I want to be."

"So she actually sold it to you?"

He nodded. It hadn't been an easy process getting it here tonight, and he'd paid four times what her daddy's truck was actually worth. But there was no reason for her to know that. "Yeah, babe. She did. Now are we going to sit here all night talking about it, or you going to take me home and have your way with me?"

His beautiful girl turned on the seat, the weathered leather beneath her groaning in protest. Knowing he'd put that light in her eyes, that best-day-of-my-life look on her face, made it well worth it. He'd have paid five times more than he did. Ten times over. He leaned over to kiss her once more. But she did something he wasn't expecting. Wrapping her hands around his neck, she yanked him to her and practically climbed on top of him. He buried his hands in her thick hair as she kissed him so hard it hurt. He groaned out loud. She was the best kind of pain. The addictive kind. He licked against her tongue and her swollen lips in the same way he liked to lick against her clit when they made love. Her sweet moan said she recognized the gesture. He hoped her daddy wouldn't haunt him from the grave for contemplating sex with his daughter in his truck.

"Thank you," she breathed when they came up for air. "I love it. I…I love you."

Time stopped and his hands let go of her even though he didn't mean for them to. His chest began to throb due to the painful punch of his heart against his ribs. *You were supposed to say it first, you fucking moron.* He closed his eyes and tried to breathe. *Say it back. Say it the hell back, Corbin.* But when he swallowed, it was as if he'd swallowed the words.

When he opened his eyes, they met her wide, shocked ones. *She didn't mean to say that. She got caught up in the moment.* He needed a drink. He needed to tell her he'd been drinking. He'd had a few after the show to ease his nerves about their date. His fists clenched because he had so much to say, and for some reason he couldn't say shit. *Tell her everything. If she still wants to be with you after that, tell her you love her back.*

"You ready for this?" Kylie asked as she turned the key in the ignition. Her sweet smile looked forced. He knew she was trying to pretend her declaration of love hadn't even happened.

Trace made himself grin back. When their gazes met, his mind went haywire. And then blank. *The ride. She means the ride.* But something in the way she was looking at him said she meant a whole lot more. And he didn't know the answer to that.

"Yeah." He leaned in for one more kiss, hoping it would ease the sting of the words he hadn't said. "Yeah, I'm ready." But he kind of wasn't. Not really.

They were about fifteen minutes outside of Macon when Trace plugged his iPod into the dock he'd installed. He scrolled to the song he liked the most so he could get Kylie's opinion on it. And because he desperately needed to do something about the impenetrable, suffocating silence that had filled the cab since they'd left Atlanta.

"Tell me what you think of this one," he said as he clicked play. She'd been quiet the entire drive. He didn't like it. He hoped music would ease the tension. The song was called *If This is Goodbye* and had been written by some unknown. Noel Davies had included it in the list of ones he wanted Trace to record and it was the only one he liked. He was surprised at how much he wanted Kylie to like it too.

A woman's voice filled the cab of the truck. *If this is goodbye, I'm gonna say what's on my mind. If this is goodbye, I wanna look you in the eye.*

Kylie took her eyes off the road briefly to glance at him. Her expression told him she was into it already.

Everybody's got a side of them that no one else can see, but the first time you looked in my eyes, I knew you saw that part of me. So if this is goodbye, if this is goodbye, I'm gonna say what's on my mind.

You may not love me the way I need you to. But as long as my heart beats, I'll still be in love with you.

So if this is goodbye, if this goodbye, I wanna kiss you one last time. 'Cause I know I'll run and hide. When I see you out, when I see you with her, when I see you walkin' down the street. I'm gonna pretend I don't notice. I'm gonna pretend it's not killin' me.

I don't want to walk away. I don't want to let you go. But you made that choice for us and it's too hard to hold on.

So if this is goodbye, if this is goodbye, I'm gonna say what's on my mind. If this is goodbye, I wanna kiss you one last time.

He turned the speakers down as the male voice began singing his part. "Well, what do you think?"

"It's a duet."

"Yeah?" Not exactly the answer he was expecting.

"It's nice. I like it. Kind of sad, but pretty. Soulful. Be a good chance for you to switch it up from the drunken party anthems."

Trace shifted, lowering his arm from where it'd been resting on the back of the bench seat. "What the hell is that supposed to mean?" He sang more than just party anthems, dammit.

Kylie laughed at him. "Actually it sounds a bit more like something Bryce Parker would sing. It's just not your usual—"

"You gotta be kidding me." He rubbed his hands roughly over his knees. Jesus, this woman knew how to press his buttons.

"Trace, I wasn't tryin' to upset you. Just doesn't sound like something you'd choose, that's all." She glanced over at him. He knew he wore his hurt on his face. "I didn't mean—"

"Forget it." Now they were even. Both hurting because they didn't get the reaction they'd been expecting.

"Excuse me?" She turned and looked at him with her forehead all scrunched.

"Never mind. I like it. Thought you might be interested in recording it together. Obviously you're not." He shrugged like it wasn't a big deal. But for some reason this hurt a lot more than it should. *Probably not as much as not hearing 'I love you' when you're expecting it, asshole.*

"Trace! Don't be a baby. I would love to—"

"Turn left at the next road," was all he said. He switched the iPod off and checked his cell phone. He had four missed calls from Gretchen and one from Pauly. Great. This night was going straight down the shitter.

"I know how to get there," Kylie said quietly.

He nodded. He wasn't trying to be a dick. Not really. It was dark and the back roads weren't exactly well lit. But his pride was wounded and he knew there was some shit going down somewhere because Gretchen was calling him again. He cursed himself for ever giving that woman his number.

"Pauly?" Kylie asked, nodding at his cell phone buzzing in his hand.

Well this wasn't going to go over well. He cleared his throat. "Gretchen."

He could tell by the way her posture stiffened that this bothered her. But her voice was even when she spoke. "That her calling now?"

"It is," he answered honestly.

"Answer it. Might be important."

He sighed. Looking down at the screen, he saw that the call had gone to voicemail. Whatever. Gretchen could figure out her own shit. He ran a hand through his hair, wishing he could start the whole night over again. "Look, I'm sorry. I don't know why that song is such a big deal. It's not. I just heard it and thought maybe we could talk about recording it. But you're right. It's not exactly my sound. But then neither is *The Other Side of Me* and that one's going to be huge, right?"

Kylie smiled tentatively at him as she turned into the driveway. "I like the song, Trace. I didn't mean to make you upset. It's just not the direction you've been going the past few years. I mean, you recorded *Goodbye in Your Eyes* like two years ago and that's the last time I've heard you singing a ballad like that. I guess *Not That Kinda' Man* sort of fits in with that though, so yeah. This could be an amazing song if you really want to do it."

It made him feel good that she followed his career. He smiled and leaned over to kiss her as she turned the truck off. "It's okay. I appreciate you being honest with—"

Before he could finish, his phone buzzed angrily in his hand. He glanced down at the same time Kylie did.

"Just answer it."

He hit accept on the screen. "Gretchen, what the hell are you-"

"You were right. I need help, Trace."

Jesus. She was a sobbing mess.

"I can't…I can't do this anymore. I don't know what to do. I'm at the hotel and I tried calling him and he won't talk to me and I've ruined everything." Her words ran together, and Trace had no idea who "he" was, but she sounded awful. Weak. Very unlike Gretchen.

"Calm down. I'll be there as soon as I can." He should've told her to get some sleep and they'd talk tomorrow. But in a way, it was a relief to have an excuse to bail. For the first time ever, he needed to put some distance between himself and the girl he loved more than anything. He wasn't mad at her at all. Not about the song and definitely not about saying she loved him. He was pissed at himself. For being unworthy. For lying this whole time about his drinking. For not being able to say what he should have when she gave him the chance. He was on edge, drowning in a sea of feelings he'd never learned to swim through, and he damn sure didn't want to take any of that out on her. But he knew he would if he didn't back off.

Gretchen sniffled and sobbed loudly. "Oh-okay. Shit. I didn't mean to ruin your night. God. I ruin everything. Trace, I'm sorry. Just—"

"Shh. Breathe, Gretch." Trace rubbed his neck, trying to ease some of the tension that was holding him so rigid it ached. It didn't work. He glanced over at Kylie. Her expression was so completely blank he knew she had to be making a pretty serious effort to keep it that way. "Try and calm down. I'll be there in a few."

After he disconnected the call, he turned towards his girlfriend. His supremely pissed off girlfriend. "Hey."

"Hey yourself," she answered, still staring straight ahead.

"Gretchen is going through some stuff and I need to go talk to her. Before she does something crazy." He took a deep breath. This was not a position he was used to being in with a woman. One where he cared so much about her being upset. He hadn't technically done anything wrong but knowing their night was ruined, the last night they'd get for five more weeks, sucked.

Kylie nodded without looking at him. "Okay."

"Babe, look at me. I don't want to go. I kind of have to." *Do I really? Is that a lie?* He wasn't sure anymore.

Finally she turned to face him "Why? What are you supposed to do about it? Why is this your problem?" The pain in her eyes made his head throb. Hurt and disappointment rolled off of her in waves. She was disa-fucking-ppointed because he had to deal with Gretchen instead of being with her. And because he couldn't just say what she needed to hear. Well, that made two of them. This was it. The other shoe was dropping. He didn't know what he'd been thinking trying to play this perfect boyfriend role. It wasn't him. It never would be.

He scrubbed a hand over his face. "It's complicated. Basically the label has decided we're a package deal. Either of us screws up, they pull the plug, and we're both gone."

He watched as she bit her lip. "Oh-kay."

"And honestly? When I was all fucked up, you were there for me. You were brave enough to be honest with me when no one else was. I kind of feel like I should pay it forward, you know?" He rubbed her leg gently, hoping to pull her closer but she didn't budge. "I won't be long."

"When will you be back?" Her usually clear voice was soft and heavy. *With hurt. You're hurting her. Again.*

"As soon as I can. Promise."

"You want me to go with you?"

"Naw. You don't need to see this." The last thing he wanted to do was drag his beautiful angel into the gutter. Hell, he wasn't even sure he could handle seeing it.

For some reason that seemed to hurt her feelings worse. "I don't mind."

"Kylie, there is no way I'm putting you through this right now. I'll calm her down and come right back."

He watched her force a smile that never made it to her eyes. "You're a good man, Trace Corbin."

No I'm not.

She leaned forward and kissed him softly on the mouth. He didn't like it. It was nothing like their usual heated kisses. It felt a hell of a lot like goodbye.

"*Open* up, Gretch. It's me." Trace pounded his fist on the hotel room door. His stomach twisted at the thought of what awaited him on the other side. Alcohol probably. And lots of it.

The door opened and Gretchen stood there, still sobbing with mascara streaking down her face. "Hey, t-thanks for coming." She stepped aside so he could come in. Strangely enough, he didn't see any telltale signs of an all-night bender anywhere. *Damn.* He'd have to go somewhere else to get a drink then. She sat on the bed and stared down at a wad of tissue in her hand.

"You're welcome. Want to tell me what the hell is going on with you?" Trace sat in a chair beside a table and waited for her to tell him what her deal was. After a few moments of sniffling, she looked up. Pain, raw and exposed, filled her eyes, her face. He needed a drink to deal with this. Women crying was his kryptonite.

"I'm ready to talk to Dr. Reynolds, Trace. The sooner, the better."

"Seriously?"

Gretchen nodded, and he breathed a huge sigh of relief. Jesus. He had no idea what the cause of Gretchen's sudden turnaround was, but he wasn't questioning it. He whipped out his phone and texted both Dr. Reynolds and Pauly to meet them first thing in the morning. Or now if possible.

When he was finished, he looked up at her. She was a woman he'd considered a friend once. And then a friend with benefits. And now just a woman who needed help. "Not that I'm not thrilled to hear that you're ready to get help, but what brought this on?"

She startled him by tearing up all over again.

"Whoa. Hell, I'm sorry. I didn't mean to—"

"I have a son," she said evenly as she wiped her eyes. Trace's heart stuttered, missed a beat, and restarted all out of rhythm. "Today is his birthday. I called but he didn't…he didn't want to talk to me."

Oh dear God. Please no. The internal plea was the closest he'd gotten to prayer since he was a kid. He forced himself to breathe deeply. The world slid off its axis and began to spin around him. "H-how old is he?"

She grinned through her tears and shook her head. "I had him two years before I even met you, Trace. He's eight."

"Oh praise God. I mean, not to be a dick, but you just scared the ever-living shit out of me."

She rolled her eyes. "Relax, you're not a daddy. Well, you might be. Who knows where the hell you've been? But you're not my kiddo's dad, so you can rest easy."

His breathing was slowly returning to normal. "So who takes care of him while you're on the road?"

Gretchen's usually hard gaze went soft as she stared at a point in the distance. "My mama. She's pretty much raised him. His dad was never in the picture and I haven't been…" She trailed off and glanced up at him with pleading eyes. "I never meant for things to get so—"

"Shh, I know, Gretch. I understand." He did. He really did. As much as Gretchen pissed him off and drove him half insane, he knew what it was like to feel like you'd given control of yourself to something else. To give up on dealing with your problems and settle for the numbness. Kylie had shown him kindness and strength, and she'd been there for him when no one else was. Maybe he could do the same thing for Gretchen.

"Dr. Reynolds is coming, okay? But I really need to get back to

Kylie. She's not exactly thrilled about me being here." He stood to leave but Gretchen reached out and touched his arm.

"Trace. Do you love her?"

His world threatened to spin again. It was a simple question. But the answer was complicated. "Yeah. Yeah, I do." He ran a hand through his hair and tried to think straight. *Why in the hell did I just tell Gretchen when I couldn't even tell her?* "I didn't even know if I was capable of that, you know? But she...she makes me feel like I'm capable of just about anything."

Gretchen tilted her chin up and stared up into his eyes. "I'm a mess. I know that. And it takes a mess to recognize one. If you love her, if you really want to have a future together, you should get some help, too."

What the hell? Trace snorted. "Don't be dramatic. I've got it under control." He slid his arm out of her grasp.

"That's what I thought, too," Gretchen whispered. "Then eight years went by."

He rolled his eyes and headed towards the door.

But the woman wasn't done apparently. "I know you're still drinking. How do you think she'd feel about that? How will you feel when she finds out?"

Her words stopped him cold. The fact that she'd said *when* not *if*.

It would be the end of my fucking world. That's how I'd feel.

Gretchen sighed as if she'd read his thoughts. "I've never been in love. Not like you and her. I saw the way you looked at each other. And yeah, I was jealous."

Trace turned and stared wide-eyed at her admission.

Gretchen rolled her eyes. "Not like that, you arrogant bastard. Just...I wish I could find that. Someone to love me like that—even though I'm damaged goods."

He swallowed hard before he spoke again. "She told me she loves me. Tonight. I bailed." *Fuck.* That look on her face was burned into his memory. The emotions flitted across so fast he barely had time to name them. Surprised, probably at her own words. Then hopeful as she waited for his response. Then bone-deep hurt when he couldn't give her what she needed.

Gretchen snorted. "Sounds like you. That girl was ready to wrestle me to the fucking ground just for looking at you. Did you really not know how she felt?"

How can anyone love me? I'm an asshole, a drunk, and on the brink of being a has-been. What's to love? He didn't know what to say so he shrugged and watched as Gretchen took a deep breath. "The thing about it is, I love my son. God, I love him so much. And I think he loves me too. At least…I hope he still does." Her eyes filled with tears and her shoulders shook with the promise of another breakdown. Somehow she managed to choke it back. "But he deserves better than who I am right now. So I am damn well going to do whatever it takes to try and be better." Gretchen paused to wipe the tears from her eyes with her fingertips. "And if you really love that girl, you'll do the same."

CHAPTER Twenty Four

It was nearly daylight when she heard him come in. She'd been fighting off sleep for hours. Waiting for a call or a text or something. But nothing ever came. He didn't turn on any lights when he came in, so she said nothing. Even though her back was to him, she was aware of his every movement. She heard him take off his watch and lay it on the night table with a heavy thud. Listened to the rustling of his clothes as he undressed. The mattress shifted beneath her as he lowered his weight onto it. He huffed out a sigh behind her back.

She focused on keeping her breathing even. Pretending to be asleep felt somewhat childish, but she'd had hours to work up plenty of hurt and pissed off about the fact that he'd left her for Gretchen. There had to have been someone else who could've handled it. And he smelled like a brewery. Talking would lead to fighting. She knew this. For once, she didn't have anything to say to him. And for some reason, she had a feeling he'd already said everything he had to say. To someone else.

When the sun finally broke in through the windows, Kylie turned to the man sleeping next to her. There were still dark circles of exhaustion ringing his eyes so she was careful not to disturb him as she got out of bed. After making a pot of strong coffee, she took her mug out to the back deck.

God, she loved this place so much. It was quiet, peaceful. Perfect. She lowered herself onto the glider swing and sipped her steaming drink. The land stretched and sprawled out before her. It was almost time to go back to the cramped bus of overflowing estrogen and she'd barely slept a few hours.

The pond wasn't visible from where she sat but she knew exactly where it was. So much for her skinny-dipping plans. A pang of sadness struck her hard and fast. She took a few deep breaths to try and stifle it, but it left a residual ache in her chest all the same. Something was going on. He didn't want her to know about it and he was cutting her out of a part of his life. The very same part Gretchen Gibson seemed to be very much a part of.

"Hey." Trace's sleepy voice interrupted her disturbing thoughts. She turned to see him standing behind her in nothing but a pair of plaid flannel pajama bottoms.

"Mornin'." She focused on her coffee instead of ogling him like she wanted to. "There's coffee. I can't make breakfast like you do, but coffee I can handle."

One corner of his mouth quirked up as he sat beside her. "I saw. Kylie, about last night—"

"Everything go okay?" she asked in a clipped tone. She was torn. Part of her wanted to demand every detail from the minute he'd left her last night until now. And part of her...just didn't want to know. Knowing might change things. In a few short hours they'd be saying goodbye for five more weeks. Seemed like a bad time to rock the boat. Especially when it felt like the slightest movement might sink the damned thing altogether.

Trace snorted. "As good as could be expected I guess. She's meeting with Dr. Reynolds this morning, so that's a good thing."

She nodded absently in agreement.

Trace angled himself so she'd have to lean back into his arms. She didn't mind. For one peacefully perfect moment she didn't care about last night. Or what anyone was saying about them online. Or anything really. This was what it felt like to be home. Loved. He might not have said the words, but the red and gray truck sitting in the driveway told her how he felt. Trace interrupted her bliss with the low rumble of his voice in her ear. "Babe? Can we talk a minute? I owe you an explanation."

Yeah, they could talk. Or they could make the most of this time before it was over. "You did something nice for a friend, Trace." She swallowed the pain calling Gretchen his friend caused. "The only thing you *owe* me is a shower."

God bless Claire Ann for sleeping in. And Rae must've been at her mom's or with friends. Thank goodness for small miracles. Kylie sat her coffee on the patio table and stood. She stared into his eyes as she unbuttoned the shirt of his she'd slept in and let it fall to her feet. She slid her panties down her legs and stepped out of them, moving towards him. "You comin'?"

His eyes were molten when they met hers. "Yes, ma'am."

She could feel him close behind her as she made her way to his bedroom. She didn't even glance at the bed for fear they wouldn't make it to the shower if she did. Without even looking at him, she stepped into the bathroom and turned the shower nozzle to hot.

At some point he must've ditched his pants. When she felt him step into the shower behind her, his erection brushed against her backside. She ached for him. Last night hurt so bad and now she needed him to heal that hurt. Smooth the jagged edges caused by spending so many hours without him, filling her the way only he could.

"Hmm." He was close enough that she felt the vibration in his chest. "Where were we?" He yanked her roughly backwards, turning her and pressing her back up against the shower wall before she had time to protest. Not that she would have. "Yeah, about here looks right."

"You fixed it," she said, nodding at the bar on the shower door she'd broken in the throes of passion last time they were here.

Trace grinned and shook his head. "Couldn't. Had the whole door replaced. Feel free to break it again. I've got one on backorder just in case." He winked, and she tilted her chin so he'd kiss her on the mouth. But he didn't. His eyes met hers for a brief second, long enough for them to convey how deeply he wanted her and how much she was going to enjoy this. It was a promise. One she was going to make sure he kept.

He palmed her face and then let his hand trail downward. He brushed past her breasts to her stomach.

She moaned out loud when he dropped to his knees. "Open up, pretty girl," he murmured against her hip. She spread her legs, twitching in anticipation as he ran his hand up her inner thigh. At the first touch of his tongue against her, she jerked and her legs tried to close. Trace gripped her inner thighs, holding them apart as his tongue lashed against her over and over again. She whimpered at the intensity of it. He wasn't slowing down or backing off. Just licking her deep and hard at a relentless pace.

When he slid a finger inside of her, she felt herself coming apart at the seams. But she wasn't ready.

She grabbed him by the hair of his head and pulled. Hard. He looked up at her, eyes wide and dark.

"Make love to me, Trace. I've waited. I've been waiting." She didn't have to wait much longer.

He stood, gripping her ass with both hands and lifting her easily. She clung to his shoulders, digging her fingers in so hard she worried a little about hurting him. But he didn't complain so she held on tighter.

When he impaled her on his thick shaft, she made loud, unapologetic sounds of pleasure. The first few were just noise. But then the moans came, and the word on her lips was her favorite one. His name.

CHAPTER Twenty Five

Watching Kylie Ryans come was like witnessing a miracle. The combination of events that occurred simultaneously was magnificent to behold. Her body stiffened and jerked around him. Her smooth, tan skin flushed and warmed. Her bright blue eyes shone even brighter than usual. Once she opened them, that was.

After they'd finished in the shower, he'd carried her to his bed, thinking she might want to rest before heading back to the bus. But when she'd hiked her leg over his waist, rubbing her satin skin again his, well, that had been the beginning of round two. "Fuck," he groaned as she clenched and pulsed around him. Her body always stroked the underside of his dick just right. She was so damn tight, the gripping and pulling of her walls pulled his orgasm from deep inside. It wasn't until after he'd finished releasing himself inside of her that he realized what they'd forgotten.

He let out a breath, collapsing on top of her. "Dammit, Kylie, I—"

"It's okay," she said softly, plowing her fingers gently through his hair.

Like hell it was okay. She'd said she wanted to use condoms and that she hadn't been doing a great job with her pill. He should've pulled out. He should be panicking. But he just didn't have the energy left to work up a good flip out.

"I'm sorry. I should've—"

"Trace." Her voice saying his name was music in the air. It was his favorite song. "It's fine. I checked last night and I've done better with my pills than I thought. I haven't missed one. Just been taking them at weird times is all."

He placed a chaste kiss on her breast just before laying his head on it. Damn, she felt good naked and in his arms. Exactly how and where he needed her. For a little while, all the voices in his head telling him why this was wrong, why it would never work, and that he'd never be good enough for her, just shut the hell up. It was pure and utter perfection. Just like she was.

A tiny thought snaked its way to the forefront of his mind. A glimmer of hope that somehow managed to wrestle its way through the deep dark pit of doubt. Maybe, just maybe, what they had, the two of them together, was perfect too.

Five weeks later, he was anxiously pacing the bus like a caged beast, anticipating seeing his girl again as they pulled into the parking lot of a bar in Charlotte. The time apart sucked and phone calls and video chats weren't soothing his urge to drink or his dick like the real live version could. He'd just hung up with her when Gretchen appeared from her room. She was makeup free and clad in jeans and a T-shirt. Her hair was pulled back and her eyes were clear. Hallelujah. The last thing he needed was to take an intoxicated Gretchen to Kylie's show. She really did seem to be making progress. It was more than he could say for himself.

"Hey," she said, coming up beside him. "Can we talk?"

He checked his watch and motioned for her to follow him off the bus. "Can we do it inside? I don't want to be late. The girls don't always perform in the same order and I don't want to risk miss—"

"I'm leaving the tour, Trace."

His feet hit the pavement and he froze. "You're what?"

Gretchen fidgeted, wringing her hands and then shrugging. "I'm going into rehab. Dr. Reynolds found this place in Dallas that's supposed to be really good. Private."

"What about the label?" They'd drop her for sure. He didn't have anyone there who'd do him any favors or he'd try to help her out. "Maybe Pauly could—"

"Trace. Listen. Please." She put a hand up to silence him. "I'm done. I'm done with the label. All of it. It's time to get my act together and be the kind of mother Daniel deserves. That's my son's name. Daniel. He likes to be called Danny." He watched as the moisture gathered in her eyes again. "Or at least he used to."

Jesus. She was breaking down again. His fiddle player's name was Danny. That probably sucked for her, hearing his name so often. He leaned over to give her a hug. He meant for it to be a quick one but she began full out sobbing in his arms. Women crying was not something he was equipped to handle. And yet, it seemed to be happening a lot lately. Any time one of his sisters or Kylie cried he felt like a helpless jackass. "Hey, it's gonna be okay. We'll talk to Dr. Reynolds inside and I bet you'll feel a lot better afterwards." He gave her a few pats and pulled back just as the flashbulb of a camera went off.

What the hell?

"Trace, Gretchen, are you two an item?" a heavy fella in a Hawaiian shirt called out as he snapped another photo.

"Get lost, asshole," Trace said, ushering Gretchen into the building. He was proud of Gretchen, he was. But things like this, some jerkoff causing problems that would just cause Kylie pain, just made him want a drink that much more.

CHAPTER Twenty Six

"That's her!"

"There she is!" The voices came just before a small herd of stampeding paparazzi converged on her and her friends.

"Shit, let's go," Mia commanded, ushering Kylie towards the entrance of The Evening Muse, a bar in Charlotte where they were performing and hosting open mic night.

Kylie gaped at the crowd gathering around her. She knew things would change after Trace kissed her in front of the world at the festival in Nashville. But she didn't expect it to be like this. A few photographers had begun accosting her before and after shows in the last few weeks. But this was the most she'd seen all together in a crazed, aggressive mob like this. Thankfully Mia and Lily flanked her, shoving her forward and forcing her feet to move.

Someone whistled loudly. It pierced the air and she winced as she tried to make her way through the crowd. The questions began pelting her like bullets.

"Kylie, do you know that Trace Corbin and Gretchen Gibson are in there? Did you ask them to come?"

"Are you and Trace really an item or is it all for publicity?"

"Kylie! Hey, over here! Kylie, do you plan to confront Trace about his night on the town with Gretchen? Have you seen the photographs of them checking into a hotel in Georgia?"

"Is Trace cheating on you with Gretchen? Or are you his little thing on the side?"

She was thankful for the aviators that hid her eyes. It was like they all knew exactly where she was most vulnerable. And the flashbulbs were bright as hell. And did someone say *hotel in Georgia*? Her stomach sank, pulling her heart down with it.

When they made it safely inside the bar, she was relieved that the voices didn't penetrate the walls. She'd never been so sick of hearing her own name. But her relief was short lived. Making her way to the stage with Mia and Lily, she caught sight of something that sent her heart pounding even harder than the paps had. Trace, Gretchen, Pauly, and a well-dressed man Kylie didn't recognize sat in a back corner table. Together. Looking like they were enjoying each other's company. Immensely.

She turned to approach them, but Mia grabbed her. Kylie eyed the girl's fingers on her upper arm before glaring up at her. "I'm going over there. He's my boyfriend and I haven't seen him in five damn weeks."

"Don't do it, seriously. Look." Mia nodded in the direction of several patrons with their phones out. They were most likely waiting for her to make a scene so they could post it all over the Internet.

"You holding me back like I'm a rabid animal isn't helping things, Mia," she bit out. "Since when do you give a shit anyways?"

"I don't." Mia dropped her hand. "Listen, don't look over there. Just smile, Kylie. They need to see you smiling. This snarling-at-the-world thing you've got going isn't endearing you to any record labels. Trust me."

"I'm sorry about screwing things up for you with BackRoom Records," Kylie said quietly. She forced a tiny smile because it was all she could manage. She followed Mia's advice and didn't look over in Trace's direction. She just…couldn't. Not with the words *hotel in Georgia* burning themselves into the back of her mind.

"And you're right. Okay, let's go."

Mia nodded and walked to the stage. Kylie followed, even though it meant walking away from the one person she usually wanted to run towards.

The show went well despite the fact that, while she was on stage, Trace barely even looked up. He glanced at her and winked a few times but the rest of the time he was deep in conversation with the members of his table. After she finished performing and introducing amateur acts with Lily and Mia, she sat with them at a table near the stage and waited for Trace to come to her. But when he finally did, she wished he hadn't.

Because he didn't come alone.

Gretchen Gibson offered Kylie an apologetic smile as she approached. "Hey. Great show y'all," she said to the three of them.

"Thanks. Wow, you're Gretchen Gibson! I'm Lily Taite. Nice to meet you." Lily and Gretchen shook hands. Mia just nodded and turned to order a drink from a nearby waitress.

Kylie steeled herself when Gretchen turned her gaze to her. "Hey, Kylie. Good to see you again."

She glanced at Trace, who rubbed his neck and gave her a small smile before she gave her full attention to Gretchen. She forced herself not to grit her teeth. "Thanks for coming."

"Thanks for inviting me."

I didn't. She nodded anyways. Shit. Gretchen was being nice. The photographers outside were shouting about hotel rooms in Georgia, and Trace seemed about as comfortable as a whore in church. Had something happened? Her daddy always said, "Where there's smoke, there's fire." Maybe the paps were onto something. The sickening realization had her stomach churning. As did the word *paps*. She hated it. Reminded her of *pap smear. No wonder celebrities refer to them that way. Seeing them is about as much fun as visiting the gynecologist.*

She felt a little better when Trace leaned forward and kissed her softly. "Hey, babe. You killed it, as always." There was still pride sparking in his eyes so she took that as a good sign.

"Trace, um, can we talk? Privately?"

He nodded.

"Yeah, hey, I'm gonna get back over there," Gretchen said before Trace could answer. "Enjoy your night, y'all."

Once she was out of earshot and Lily and Mia had gone to sit at a table with the people from one of the local radio stations, Kylie stared up at Trace. She hoped her eyes were conveying her question of *What in God's name is going on?* So she wouldn't have to ask out loud.

"Listen, Kylie, I know lately things have been a little—"

"Kylie! We need you over here!" Lily's arm was waving wildly in the air as she motioned her over.

"Just a sec," Kylie shouted back.

"Trace, the guys outside said something about—"

"Trace Corbin!" a high-pitched female voice squealed. "Oh my God! Oh my God! I can't believe you're here! We heard you might be! That's why we came! Can we please get a picture with you?"

Normally, Kylie would've rolled her eyes at the redhead and her friends. But she was almost grateful for the interruption, so she just stepped back and made room for them to get into the picture. "Here, I'll take it," she offered. The girl handed her a phone and Kylie took the picture of Trace with each of his arms wrapped around two girls. For a second, she couldn't stop staring at the image on the hot pink encased iPhone. This was Trace. This was who he wanted to be. Not some guy chilling with her on Friday nights at the farm.

She returned the phone but the girls weren't done. Not even close.

They were fawning all over Trace, asking him to sign everything from their phones to their boobs. Kylie shook her head. "I have to do this radio interview," she told him, unsure if he could hear her over the music and the girls.

"Okay," he answered as he signed the ass of some blond girl's jeans. "We'll talk when you're done."

By the time she'd finished her interview the place was packed.

She couldn't see Trace anywhere in the crowd. She excused herself from the table where Mia and Lily were still chatting up the radio host and made her way to the bar. Shoving through sweaty bodies was not her idea of a fun night. When she finally made it, she still hadn't found him. A decent looking clean-cut guy in a yellow polo shirt was sitting on the stool next to where she stood.

"Hey, can I borrow this for a sec?" she asked, gesturing to his stool.

He took a long pull from his bottle of Budweiser and turned to her. "Hm, well, I'm using it right now. What do you need it for?"

She gave her best flirty grin. "I can see that, darlin'. I'm just trying to find my...friend. He disappeared on me."

Yellow Shirt leered at her. "Well I'm here now. I'm sure your *friend* will be just fine on his own."

Oh for the love of bacon. Why did guys have to be so damned obnoxious?

"You know what, never mind." She turned to find another opening where she could maybe see a little better. Just as she turned to walk away, a hand grabbed her arm, yanking her backward.

"Don't be like that, sweetheart. Stay, relax. I'll buy you a drink while you wait for your *friend*."

"No, thank you," Kylie said through clenched teeth. She tried to jerk her arm from Yellow Shirt's grip but he wasn't letting go. Suddenly the crowd seemed to be surging towards the bar and she couldn't breathe. Or move.

"Hey, buddy, the lady said no thanks," a guy said from behind her. She half-hoped it would be Trace but it wasn't. It was a heavyset man in overalls.

"Mind your own business," the guy holding her said. His voice was no longer friendly but practically a growl. "About that drink—"

Kylie didn't let him finish. She grabbed the glass of whiskey Overalls was drinking and splashed it into Yellow Shirt's face. "I said no thank you." She yanked her arm back and leaned close to overalls. "I'll buy you another," she promised, reaching into her pocket to grab what little bit of cash she carried.

"You fucking bitch," Yellow Shirt shouted in her face. Before she got the money out, a fist swung by her head and Overalls had laid Yellow Shirt out. She ducked as the shouting began. Someone shoved her and she nearly fell on her ass.

"Guess they don't teach you college boys how to talk to ladies," Overalls said as he stood.

"Kylie!" someone shouted. Probably Mia. Or Lily. She wasn't sure.

The next thing she knew, Trace was wrapping his arms around her and shielding her from the madness. Yellow Shirt was back up, and apparently he had friends. Two other guys stood on either side of him and they all looked ready to murder someone.

"What the hell is going on here?" Trace demanded.

"He wanted to buy me a drink, I declined, and–"

"And he grabbed her," Overalls broke in.

"*Who* grabbed her?" Trace said, turning to glare at Yellow Shirt and his friends. Kylie saw the veins throbbing in his neck. This was not a good sign.

"No one. Forget it. Let's just go." She wrapped her arms around his waist and tugged. Hard.

"One in the yella," Overalls so helpfully offered.

Trace broke her grip and cocked his fist. Before she even had time to yell at him to stop, he'd cracked the other guy in the mouth. One of Yellow Shirt's friends swung at Trace and missed, grazing Overalls. Overalls grabbed the guy and shoved him roughly against the bar.

"Fight!" someone shouted, and that was the last thing she heard before she saw the black T-shirt pulled taut over the broad chest of a bouncer blocking her vision.

"Break it up!" the muscle-covered man shouted. She was shoved a few more times before uniformed officers converged on them. The bouncer had Trace wrapped in a bear hug. Kylie felt tears stinging in her eyes at the sight of him looking so angry and being held back. This was all her fault. The media and the label were going to give him so much hell. All because of her. Because whatever band was playing obviously thought this was a time to be funny, they struck up a song she knew was called *Read Me My*

Rights. Awesome.

"It wasn't them," Overalls was shouting to the taller of the two male cops. "It was him." He pointed at Yellow Shirt and his friends. Two of them were bleeding. Trace wasn't. *This does not look good.*

"Let's take this outside," the shorter, stockier officer said. He looked like he'd just gotten out of the military and was itching to kick some ass himself. Kylie followed the bouncer and the officers as Trace, Overalls, Yellow Shirt, and his friends were guided out the back exit. She could practically hear the phones recording the whole thing. "Get the hell out of here," the cop shouted at a guy with an expensive-looking camera who was waiting by the back exit. He left, but not before firing off a few shots of all of them.

Kylie stood close to Trace's side. He wrapped an arm around her and she looked up. His expression was calm but she could still see his jaw clenching and his pulse throbbing in his neck.

"Okay, folks. So what the hell happened in there?" the taller cop asked. Yellow Shirt and his friends piped up right away, saying they were attacked for no reason. Trace's grip tightened on her as they waited for them to finish.

"Wait a minute. Not all at once." The officer said a few things into a blaring speaker on his shoulder and pointed at Kylie. "You. Blondie. What happened in there?"

She took a deep breath, sure her voice would shake. She wasn't scared of cops and had always managed to charm her way right out of traffic tickets and even a few underage drinking incidents back during the days of field parties in high school. But she was terrified for Trace. An arrest would probably get his tour canceled and he'd be dropped from Capital Letter Records before either of them could blink. "Um, I asked to borrow his chair." She paused to point at Yellow Shirt. "And he got rude about it. He grabbed my arm and I threw a drink in his face so he'd let go." She glanced at Overalls. He was just a good ol' cornbread-fed country boy. No need to get him in trouble just for trying to help. "He told the guy to settle down, and the next thing I knew, punches were being thrown every which way. Trace tried to break it up but it just got worse." *Because he punched the dude in the face.*

The tall cop rubbed his eyes. "Okay. That sound about right?" He glanced over at Yellow Shirt and his friends. They mumbled a few things she couldn't make out but no one outright called her a liar. The cop nodded. "Good. Anyone want to press charges?"

Yellow Shirt opened his mouth but one of his friends shook his head and said something in his ear.

"All right then. It's the end of my shift and I'm not in the mood to fill out a shit-ton of paperwork at the moment. But if we have to come back, or if any officers have to come back tonight because of any of you, I'll make sure each and every one of you spends the rest of the night in lock-up. Clear?"

Everyone nodded as the officer made a point of making eye contact with each of them. Even Trace seemed subdued.

"Okay, get the hell out of my sight then."

The younger guys ambled off down the alley. Overalls shook Trace's hand and winked at Kylie. "You don't have to buy me another drink, sweetheart. Pleasure was all mine."

The taller officer made his way over to them. "Hey, folks. Sorry for the hassle back there. This place is in an odd spot. College kids and townies don't always mix well. Not the first fight we've broken up tonight."

Trace nodded and shook his hand as well. "No problem, officer. Just doing your job."

"Yeah, uh. About that." The man coughed into his hand. Kylie felt her nerves winding up all over again. "So, my girlfriend is a big fan and I hate to ask but—"

Trace cut him off with warm laughter. "Sure, man. You got a pen?"

Relief washed over her as she watched Trace sign his name on the small pad of paper the cop handed him.

Once the officers left, Kylie looked up at Trace. "That could've been really bad. I'm sorry."

"You're sorry? Kylie, the only person that could've been really bad for was you. You're the one just starting out. An arrest record is not something that draws in labels."

"Trace, you told me that Capital said any more trouble and

they'd be done with you."

He leaned forward, backing her up against the brick building and bracing one arm beside her head. She shivered when he placed his other hand on her waist. "Babe, there are other labels. I'd live. I'm just sorry I wasn't there when you needed me."

"I was looking for you," she said, annoyed at how small her voice was.

He leaned down to kiss her on the head. "I'm here now."

She wanted to ask about what the pap had said. Wanted to ask what the hell he was doing chatting it up with Gretchen instead of watching her show. More than any of that, she wanted to ask if they were going to talk about her saying she loved him and him not saying it back. But their relationship didn't always allow for long, drawn out question and answer sessions. And thank the Powers That Be he wasn't currently under arrest. So she stood on her tiptoes and pressed her mouth to his.

When the kiss ended, much too soon for her liking, Trace looked her in the eyes. "I know there's been a lot going on and we have a lot to talk about. But I'll see you next week in Nashville, okay? We'll have dinner again and talk about…everything."

"Trace, I checked your schedule. That's a lot of extra driving—"

"Hey, stop that. There's nothing that can keep me from being there. I'll be at your last show, Kylie Lou. That's a promise."

CHAPTER Twenty Seven

"Do eyes deceive me, or is that Kylie I-break-into-private-rooms-in-bars Ryans?" The voice was male. And familiar.

She turned to see a dark-haired tatted-up guy with bright blue eyes walking towards her. One either side of him was two other guys she'd never seen before.

"Who's that?" Mia asked from beside her.

"Dang, Ryans. You know all the hot boys," Lily declared.

Kylie grinned when she recognized him. Chicago had been a bust. Hardly anyone had shown up to see them. To add insult to injury, she'd seen more than one website blasting the news of Trace's near arrest today alone. A familiar face was exactly what she needed. "Steven Hero-For-a-Night Blythe. What the heck are you doing in Chicago?" Kylie squealed as she gave him a hug.

"He can be my hero for a night," Lily mumbled under her breath. Kylie discreetly jammed an elbow into her ribs once Steven released her.

"You're not the only one on tour, you know," he said, stepping back from their hug. " 'Cept you got a sponsor and a cool bus, and we cram into my shitty van."

Kylie laughed. "Y'all playin' somewhere tonight? Can we come?"

Steven grinned. "We're at Martyr's tonight if you ladies want to catch the show. We're heading there now." He nodded up the strip. "But, um, maybe lose your stalkerazzi first." He jerked his head to the other side of the street where a man in a black shirt was trying to look casual despite the giant camera hanging around his neck.

"Great." Kylie rolled her eyes and made sure to turn her back to the creepo. "Sorry, I should have introduced y'all. Steven, this is Mia Montgomery and Lily Taite," she said, gesturing to each of them.

"Hey. Steven Blythe," he drawled, shaking each of their hands. Kylie didn't miss the way his eyes lingered on Mia. Boy was such a player. But it was still nice to see someone she knew. Or sort of knew anyways. "This is Chris McGhenis. He's our lead singer." The tall, muscular blond guy stepped forward and nodded. "And my cousin, BJ. He plays the drums." BJ was short and slender and had more piercings in his ears than Kylie did.

"Nice to meet y'all," Kylie said, nodding at the other two before returning her attention to Steven. "Hey, what happened to the other guy? Ben something?"

Steven pulled a face and gave a slight shake of his head. "Decided life on the road wasn't for him, crazy bastard got married. So my man Chris took his place."

"Ah, gotcha." Out of the corner of her eye Kylie saw the photographer crossing the street, coming closer to them. "Let's go before this guy gets any more photos of us."

"Yeah, I'd rather your boyfriend not punch me again." Steven laughed, but his tone was serious.

"Sorry about that." Kylie sighed. "I'm not sure he'd really care much anymore. He's got his hands full at the moment."

Steven side-eyed her as they walked. "Yeah, I heard he was on tour with Gretchen Gibson. She's a piece of work."

"More like a piece of trash," Mia muttered.

Kylie glanced over to where Mia was. Were they on the same side about something for once? Or did Mia just hate everyone equally?

Lily was behind them, chatting up BJ and Chris like they'd asked for her life story.

"It's not just her. The whole dating while on the road on separate tours thing is just…hard."

"I bet," Steven said, nodding like he understood. "I mean, that's kind of why I don't date. I know I can't be anyone's boyfriend right now. Hell, I barely know what zip code I'm going to be in from one day to the next."

"Finally, someone speaks sense," Mia said, shooting a pointed look at Kylie. As much as Kylie hated to admit it, she was probably right. But what she had with Trace was…different. She couldn't explain it. But doing all of this without having him to share it with would seem strange. Every goal she reached would be an empty victory if he wasn't there cheering her on. Believing in her. Supporting her. Maybe even loving her. One day. A girl could dream.

"I try," Steven said as he stopped walking. "Okay, here we are. Y'all don't have to pay the cover. I'll just tell them you're with us. Here." He handed Mia the guitar case he'd been carrying. "Now you're roadies."

"Ugh," Mia groaned under the weight and shoved the case back at him. "I'd rather pay the cover."

Steven laughed, his bright eyes gleaming. "I'll take care of it. Guys should always pay on the first date anyways."

"This definitely isn't a date," Mia informed him, reaching into her pocket for what Kylie presumed was money.

Steven smirked at her just before he nodded at the man at the door. Mia glared back. They were all permitted inside without paying the cover.

Once they'd found a seat and the guys had taken the stage, Kylie arched a brow at Mia. "So, what do you think of Steven?" Judging from the heated exchange she'd just witnessed, she'd be willing to bet there was a mutual attraction forming.

Mia lowered herself into the seat between her and Lily. "Seems about as arrogant and obnoxious as the rest of '." She ordered a beer and sighed. "Tattoos are kind of hot though."

"Agreed," Lily piped up with a sigh. "And how sexy are the other two? I could write a whole album about the drummer's eyes."

Mia snorted in perfect time with Kylie's eye roll. "Jesus, Lily. You just made me throw up in my mouth."

Kylie was still smiling at Mia's comment as she ordered Cokes for her and Lily.

Hero for a Night began rocking out a Johnny Cash cover. Shitty mood or not, Kylie barely fought the urge to jump up and dance. "They're great, right?" she said, nodding her head to the beat.

"They're okay." Mia took her beer from the waitress, practically downed it in one swallow, and signaled for another.

"Dude, maybe slow down a bit. For someone not into Steven, he sure does seem to be getting you all hot and bothered."

Mia shot her a dirty look but said nothing as the band played on. The next song was catchy but in an odd way. The lyrics were familiar, but they were playing them at a slower pace than she was used to. "Is this a rap song?" she asked the two girls at her table.

Lily nodded. "It's Bruno Mars. They just country-fied it."

Kylie watched as the crowd began filling the area in front of the band. Damn, they were really good. If they weren't signed, how in the world did she stand a chance? She sipped her drink and tried not to worry about it. But a nagging thought kept returning. Was Mia right? Was the only reason she was getting any attention or respect in the industry because of Trace?

Steven stepped up to one of the mics and his words interrupted her. "We'd like to play something new we've been working on. Hope y'all enjoy it."

The drums tingled to life and Chris's hypnotic voice began singing about the pain of losing the prettiest girl in the world.

Kylie was mesmerized. She couldn't wait to tell Trace how good they were. Maybe he had some connections and could hook them up with a manager and maybe even his label. Or maybe not. His label sounded kind of shady the more she learned about it.

Mia ordered another beer and Kylie kicked her under the table. "You order one more and we'll be carrying you out of here.

Or we could get Steven to do it."

"Shut it, Oklahoma." Mia leaned forward and her dark green eyes met Kylie's. "Seriously though. Did you and him ever hook up?"

Kylie leaned back to look at her. "Steven? No. We actually only hung out once and I had too much to drink. He helped me to a bathroom and Trace got the wrong idea."

"Ah." Mia kept her face blank, but Kylie thought she saw relief in her eyes.

"You think he's cuuuuttee," she sing-songed. "You want to kiiisss him, and looovvee him, and maaarrrry him."

Mia scoffed. "You've been hanging out with Lily too long."

The girl turned from the stage at the sound of her name. "What's that supposed to mean?"

Kylie barely stifled a laugh at Lily's pouty expression.

When the song ended, Mia began heckling the band. "Play something that doesn't suck," she shouted, lifting her beer.

"Mia!" Kylie hissed at her.

Surprisingly, Steven was grinning. He stepped back up to the mic beside the lead singer. "Ladies and gentlemen, we have a special treat for you this evening."

A sinking feeling hit Kylie's stomach so hard she gripped the table.

"Mia Montgomery, our very own American Idol, is in the crowd tonight. Let's see if we can get her up here. Shall we? Come on up here, Mia. Pretty please?"

Whistles and cheers filled the darkened room. Kylie and Lily stared at Mia. The blood had drained from her face but she grinned. She finished off her most recent bottle of beer and stood. Kylie was nearly overcome with déjà vu. Damn musicians.

"Lucky girl," Lily muttered. But Kylie knew the truth. She knew Mia's heart was likely pounding a mile a minute and that she was probably secretly terrified of making a complete ass of herself. She'd been there.

Once Mia reached the stage, Chris reached out and helped her up. He gave her a big smile but shook his head at Steven. "This one's for you, Mia," Steven said into the mic. When the opening chords of Jet's *Cold Hard Bitch* began playing, Kylie covered her mouth with her hand. Steven Blythe must have balls of steel. Or at least she hoped he did. Because Mia was probably going to kick him in them.

Much to her surprise, Mia sang right into the mic along with him. And then she began doing an extremely sexy dance that involved grinding all over Chris. Which Steven's face said he didn't like one damn bit.

"Let's go," Lily said, standing and holding her hand out to Kylie. "Come on. It'll be fun."

Kylie followed her and they joined the band on stage. She imitated Mia's sexy moves on Steven—poor guy needed some TLC since Mia was hurting his feelings. Lily was head-banging with the drummer, and the whole thing was getting the crowd really riled up.

When it was over, Steven gave Kylie a hug and a kiss on the cheek. "Thanks, Ryans," he murmured in her ear. "I owe you one." She smiled and the girls hopped off the stage.

The band jumped right into another song as they returned to their seats. "Seriously, they are freaking amazing." Lily's eyes were shining as she shouted over the music.

"Yeah, they are really good," Kylie agreed.

"They're all right."

Kylie smirked over at Mia. "Is this how you get when you like a guy? 'Cause I gotta say, it's not nearly as deceiving as you probably think it is."

Mia's eyes narrowed. "Looked like he was more interested in you than me, Oklahoma."

Kylie nearly choked on her Coke. "Are you serious? That whole thing was for you. To get you up there. Someone's got a crush."

"I do not," Mia argued. But her face turned red enough to be noticeable.

Kylie raised a brow. "Yeah, I was talking about him. But methinks you doth protest too much, my friend."

Mia snorted. "Oh hell. Redneck quoting Shakespeare. The

apocalypse is upon us."

"Funny. And you can kiss my redneck ass, by the way." Kylie held her glass up and tipped it in her direction. "You know, I actually don't hate either of you nearly as much as I thought I would."

Lily's light eyes went wide as she tore them from the stage. "You thought you were going to h-hate us?"

Mia snickered. "She's a bitch, Lily. She can't help it. She has no filter. She just says whatever the hell comes into that head of hers."

Back to the Kylie Ryans Hatefest. Kylie winked at Lily. "I yam what I yam." She'd decided she was officially done letting Mia get to her.

"Is it weird that you two might be the only friends I have?" Lily asked. Kylie felt her mouth drop open. Were they friends?

"Yeah, I'm not exactly drowning in them myself," Mia said softly.

Shocker, Kylie thought but didn't say.

"Me either," Lily added quietly. "Not real ones anyways. Just the ones that want me to buy them stuff and invite them to parties."

"Well, you don't have to buy us shit," Mia informed her. "But the party invites…"

Chapter Twenty Eight

"Thank you, Columbus! Y'all are beautiful!" Trace shouted as he walked off stage with his band and a few security guys.

"Hey, you meeting with Dr. Reynolds tonight?" Mike asked as they headed towards the bus.

"Hadn't planned on it. Why, you having a hard time, man?" Trace stopped walking, letting Danny go on ahead of them. He'd been so caught up in Gretchen's mess during the tour that he'd barely had time to check in with Mike. He was three years sober but knew guys who'd fallen off after much longer than that.

"Nah, I'm good actually. Uh. Shit. Not to get all gay on you or anything, but I'm kind of worried about you."

"Me? Why?" Trace cleared his throat. Yeah, he'd had a few drinks here and there. He'd even blacked out a few nights, but for the most part he had it under control. At least that was what he kept telling himself.

Mike ran a hand through his long hair. "You just seem... wound up lately. Like any little thing is going to set you off. This can't be easy, dealing with Gretchen's bullshit and the label, and—"

Trace held a hand up. "Dude. Relax. I'm fine." He just needed to get laid. And the only girl who could give him what he needed was touring all over the country at the moment. So was he for that matter.

Mike glanced from side to side before he spoke again. "Tray, you know I mind my own business, right?"

Trace nodded. He knew he was lucky that the guys in his band had not only stuck with him but had kept their mouths shut about some of the hell he'd put them through.

"Okay, so I'm just gonna lay it all out there. I know where you are, man. You're at that place where you know you shouldn't want a drink but you do. Where it's all you can think about sometimes and giving in to the urge is a hell of a lot easier than fighting it."

Trace clenched his jaw. This would be a great time for Mike to go back to minding his own damn business.

"If you get online anytime soon for any reason at all, you're gonna see something that shoves you right over the fucking edge. I don't want that. The guys don't want that. I know Gretchen's got alcohol on that bu—"

"What the hell are you talking about, man?"

He watched as his bass player took a deep breath. "Danny and some of the guys keep tabs on your girl. Not to be shady or anything. She was just a tough chick and we're all happy to see her doing well for herself, you know?"

Trace noticed some dark silhouettes coming towards them. Roadies. "Shh." He nodded and told them thanks as they began loading equipment on the surrounding trucks. Once they were out of earshot, he turned back to Mike. "I have no idea where you're going with this. Did something happen to Kylie? Is she okay?"

He knew she was in Chicago tonight. Not the safest city on the planet. He'd made her promise not to go walking off and sightseeing alone. Not that she would necessarily listen.

"Yeah, man. She's fine. But ever since y'all went public there's been some shit going around. You know how it is. Frankly, none of us really pay any attention to any of it. But I know you. And I know you're already holding on to your sobriety with an inch of your life." Mike dropped his shoulders and held his hands up.

"Naw, screw it. I know you're still drinking. I can fucking smell it on you right now. You need to stay off the damned Internet. For a while at least."

Well now he was just getting pissed off. This was bullshit and he really wasn't in the mood. "It's probably nothing, just like the promo shots of me and Gretchen were nothing. I'll check it out and give her a call to clear things up if need be."

"Okay. I hope you're right. Can I come hang with you on the bus for a while?"

Trace raised both his eyebrows at the man across from him. Since when did Mike get all mother hen on him?

The two of them got on the bus and headed straight to the media room. Trace retrieved the bottle of water he'd crammed into the back pocket of his jeans and took a swig before he sat. He flipped open the MacBook and typed in his password. Opening the Internet browser, her smirked at Mike. Dude looked like he was waiting for the results of a pregnancy test. "Relax. I'm good." He'd learned a long time ago not to believe the shit people said about you when you were in this business. Couldn't even trust his own mother for God's sakes.

He was planning to click the page he had marked for Kylie's tour blog. But as soon as his homepage came up, he saw what Mike was so worried about.

KYLIE RYANS MOVES ON FROM TRACE CORBIN'S BETRAYAL—WITH A YOUNGER MAN.

You won't catch Kylie Ryans crying over the news that her favorite country music man is shacking up with his new co-headliner, Gretchen Gibson. But we did catch her in Chicago tonight with fellow up-and-comer... If he wanted to read the rest, he'd have to click the link for the full article. And he damn sure didn't want to do that.

Below the headline was a grainy photo of him and Gretchen saying goodbye at the hotel in Georgia. Next to it was one of Kylie walking down the street with a guy. The guy had his arm around her and she was laughing. She looked much happier than she had the last time he'd seen her. When he'd lost his temper and almost gotten them both arrested. Below the photos was a video link. He clicked it and instantly wished like hell he hadn't.

There she was. In a bar. Dancing all over Steven motherfucking Blythe. She'd never danced on him like that. He closed the video and glanced back at the photo. Same tattoos, same mess of black hair on his head. Fuck.

They'd met at The Texas Player's Club. He remembered. She'd come into the VIP room with Steven close behind. Or did they know each other before? She'd never mentioned it and he'd never asked. His fist clenched. To hell with this. He slammed the computer shut.

Mike was on him in an instant. "Okay, now you're the one who needs to relax."

"I am relaxed." He took a few deep breaths to calm his pounding heart. He felt his jaw clench and flex. "It is what it is. She can hang out with anyone she wants. I'm not her fucking keeper."

"Okay," Mike said warily. "So you're cool and you're not going to drink?"

"Naw, I'm good," he lied. "But thanks for the high school girl intervention. Much as I'd love to stay up late so you can paint my fingernails and shit, I'm going to take a shower and get some sleep."

"You hungry? We're gonna grab some burgers at a local joint before we head out."

"I'm good. Thanks though."

"Seriously. Come with us. You need to get some air."

Trace glared up at him. "You're replaceable. It'd take one phone call."

The other guy shook his head. "Corbin, don't do this. Call Dr. Reynolds. Take a walk. Call her and find out what's going on. Don't sit here and work yourself up and end up drink—"

"Get the fuck off my bus, Mike. If you want to keep your job, that is."

He gave his bass player exactly one minute to clear off the bus before he pulled up the pictures again. And that video. Jesus Christ that video. He glared at the screen until his eyes burned.

When he couldn't take any more, he slung the computer into the cabinets across from him. The noise wasn't nearly as satisfying as what he craved. He stood, not to retrieve the computer, but to grab a bottle from his liquor cabinet. Which was empty. *No way I drank them all.* Someone had taken his liquor. Except the only person who'd ever done that hadn't been on his bus in over a month. He closed his eyes, planning to count, to do some deep breathing. To try and remember how in the hell he'd gone through that many bottles of bourbon without realizing it. But all he saw was the girl he loved in another man's arms. Her body pressed against his for the world to see.

This was his fault. He knew that. He deserved this. For not telling her he loved her when he had a chance. For not ever saying the words she needed to hear to know it was him and her and no one else. He'd never be able to erase those images from his mind. Not without help. So he headed into Gretchen's room.

"*If* you wanted to see my panties, all you had to do was ask." Her low, throaty voice interrupted his search.

He slammed the dresser shut and glared at her. "Where is it? I know you have some."

"I have no idea what you're talking about." She widened her eyes, feigning an innocence she wasn't capable of. She was still worked up and sweaty from performing. Or maybe from screwing a roadie. He didn't know and he didn't care.

"Just tell me where it is, dammit!" He'd turned the entire bus upside down looking for her stash.

Gretchen stepped towards him. "What the hell is your problem? I told you, I'm not going to fuck up any more shows or whatever the hell you're worried about. I'm going to do the best I can before I leave for Dallas. I've been talking to Dr. Reynolds and—"

"I'm not worried about you," he said, immediately wishing he'd kept his mouth shut. That would've been the perfect way to play it. Like he was just confiscating her alcohol for her own good. Not because he needed a drink more than his next breath. The images of Kylie laughing as she strolled down the street with Steve, a kid he'd known since the little fucker was in middle school, were assaulting the shit out of him. The memory of what he'd seen, her writhing and grinding on him while he played guitar on stage, was driving him fucking mad. They were the kind of images a man couldn't shake. Or forget. Unless he burned them out with hard liquor.

"What's going on, Tray?" Gretchen took another step closer. She hadn't called him Tray in years. He didn't like it.

"Nothing. I'm just…getting the alcohol off the bus. Removing temptation." He ran a hand through his hair.

"Hmm. Temptation. Now there's something I can understand." She advanced on him until they were close enough to touch. "I don't know what has you all worked up, but I'd be happy to help you—"

"The only thing I want *help* with is finding where you're hiding your liquor. I know it's in here somewhere."

Gretchen cocked her head. "You really trying to get rid of it, or you just have a hankerin' for a drink?"

His face must've given him away because she smiled before he answered. Moving past him, she leaned over behind her bed. He knew she was taking her time to make sure he got a nice long view of her ass. His patience was running out. "Just give it to me."

"I'd be happy to *give it to you*," she said, licking her lips as she handed over the dark bottle. It was a half-empty pint of Jack. Or half-full, depending on how you looked at it. *Thank fuck.*

"Pass." Trace took the bottle greedily and all but ran from her room.

CHAPTER Twenty Nine

Trace's song, *Waitin' for You to Call,* was playing in her dream. They were singing it together at the Rum Room. His stormy eyes were bearing down into hers and she just wanted to grab him and hold on tight.

Softly, she began humming the tune in her sleep.

"Answer your fucking phone, Oklahoma," Mia's sleepy voice demanded.

Her eyes flew open. Where the hell was she?

She sat up and glanced around. Oh yeah, she was in a hotel room in Chicago with Mia and Lily. They'd had a cot brought up but Mia had been out with Steven and his band so Kylie and Lily got dibs on the beds. Obviously Mia had come in too tired to care where she slept because she was in bed with Lily. Trace's song was still playing. The alarm clock on the nightstand read 3:46. She grabbed her phone, yanking it free of the charger and praying everything was okay.

"Hello?" she said quietly as to not wake Lily or piss Mia off further.

"Hello yourself."

"Trace? Are you okay?" She sat up and put her feet on the floor. Except the floor grunted and moved. She squealed.

"Shh, calm down," Mia hiss-whispered. "They were sleeping in their van so I told them they could bunk with us tonight. Chris got the cot and the other two are on blankets on the floor. You just stepped on Steven probably."

"Great."

"What's great?" Trace asked, slurring his words a bit as he did. Jesus, was he drunk? The likelihood that he'd been out drinking with Gretchen made her feel woozy, and she stumbled once more in the darkness.

"Um, I just tripped over Steven. Or someone."

"What?" He was full out roaring at her now.

"Nothing. Never mind. What's going on, babe? Is something wrong?" She stepped carefully over the bodies in the floor and made her way into the bathroom. She closed the door behind her and turned on the fan so everyone wouldn't hear her conversation.

"Let's see. What could possibly be wrong? Well, for one, I had the pleasure of watching you shake your ass all over *Steven* online. And now he's in your hotel room in the middle of the fucking night. So maybe *you* can tell *me* what's going on, Kylie."

Oh, this was bad.

"Um, well we ran into—"

"You know what? Why don't I tell you how it looks from my end instead? Because to me, it looks like you're pissed that I had to deal with Gretchen when I should've been paying attention to you. So now you're making sure you get my full attention by fucking someone else. The pictures were great, by the way, but you outdid yourself with the video."

She literally seethed in anger. It rose up inside of her, lighting her on fire from her feet to her head. She ground her teeth together and did her best to keep her voice down. "I don't know what in God's name you're talking about. But I do know that if you ever accuse me of fucking anyone else, then we will be done. That's bullshit and you know it. I've only been with you. Ever. If you want to talk about people with a history of fucking anyone who—"

"Wow, resorting to throwing my past in my face. Nice. Clearly you have nothing to hide."

"I *don't* have anything to hide, thank you very much. What the hell is wrong with you? Are you drunk?"

For a moment, the other end of the line was silent and she worried he'd hung up. Adrenaline was pumping through her so fiercely she knew she'd never get back to sleep. Damn him.

"What makes you think I'm drunk?" he asked, his voice slightly softer than before.

"You're slurring your words…and you're being that guy again. The one you were before." Sobs began to choke her. This was her worst nightmare. They were miles apart and he was drunk. On a bus with another woman. One who looked at him like he was filet mignon and she was starving to death.

"I've always been that guy, Kylie Lou. Always will be."

Tears gathered in her eyes, blurring her vision. Not that she could see much in the dark anyways. "No, Trace. That's not true. You've been better—things have been better. Haven't they?" Had they? She didn't know really, since she'd hardly seen him.

"No they haven't," he said, clearing his throat loudly in the phone.

"I'll call the Vitamin Water people and tell them I need a few days to deal with a personal issue. I'm going to meet you wherever you are and we can talk about everything in person. Just please, please don't drink anymore tonight, okay?"

"No." His voice was hard and eerily calm.

Dread skittered across her skin and the blood rushed from her head. She clutched the counter for support. "No I can't come or no you won't stop drinking?"

"Both," he said just before the line went dead.

When Mia and Lily appeared in the doorway and the light flipped on, she was crouched on the closed toilet seat. Violent sobs racked her body until it was hard to breathe. She'd tried so hard to keep them quiet as to not wake the others. Obviously it hadn't worked. Yet another thing she'd failed at.

"Kylie?" Lily whispered. "You okay?" She looked up to see the girl's face bathed in fluorescent light and shock.

Happy now? Now I'm the one crying in the damned bathroom. She'd been the strong one. She'd been the calm one. She'd been the one to comfort everyone else. To take the insults and the hatred aimed at her without flinching. And now she was the one falling the fuck apart.

"What did he do?" Mia asked, barely loud enough to hear.

Kylie swiped her hands across her face, as if removing the evidence of her breakdown would help anything. "N-Nothing. He just saw some pictures and a video someone posted of us tonight and he got…" She was interrupted by her own shuddering sob. "Upset."

"I shouldn't have invited the guys to stay tonight. I'm sorry." Mia's pained expression said the apology was genuine.

She waved her hand before using it to wipe her eyes and nose again. "It wasn't just that. I mean, it didn't help, but you couldn't have known. But if anyone finds out they stayed then…" God. She didn't even want to think about what the media would say. Or how it would affect Trace. Or poor Steven. She was hazardous to everyone apparently.

She took the Kleenex Lily had pulled from the dispenser on the bathroom sink. Looking up into their worried sympathetic faces, she felt pathetic. She'd become the lovesick friend crying over a man. *Dreams do come true.*

"Was he drinking?"

Kylie felt her nerves prickling at Mia's question. But it was a fair one. She did her best to shrug. "I think so."

"Did he break up with you?" Lily asked, her eyes becoming moist as if this really mattered to her.

The words seared a hole into her chest. Because she didn't know the answer. She blew her nose into the Kleenex. "I don't know. He didn't *say* that exactly, but he was mad. Like, raging mad." *And drunk. And he's not answering my calls,* she thought but didn't say out loud. "Go back to bed. I'm fine. I'm going to get cleaned up and get some rest." She stood, thankful that they nodded and turned to leave. But she wasn't fine. Nowhere near it actually.

"*Kylie*, just call Cora and have her release a statement saying you have the flu and had a bad reaction to the medicine." Mia was steering her away from the stage. She'd bombed. Bad. Her first few songs had gone okay. Then she'd gotten distracted by a guy in a blue plaid shirt in the crowd and whiffed on her own lyrics. "Me and Lily will close together. You've done it for us, we can do it for you."

"I-I'm okay. I'm fine." She pulled her phone from the pocket of her jeans. Nothing. Not a single call or 'I'm sorry' text from him. Just their faces pressed together in the picture she'd taken the night of their date in Atlanta.

"You keep saying that. But you're one of the best performers I've ever seen. I say that because it's true. I don't even fucking like you, so I won't bother lying to make you feel better. You were a robot out there. Or a zombie. Or a zombie robot. Shit, I don't know, but that was bad."

"Gee, thanks." She sighed. Why wouldn't he just freaking call already? Couples fought. It was a part of life. But she had some things to say, dammit. And she wouldn't be able to think of anything else until she said them. She dialed his number again and it went straight to voicemail.

Mia snatched her phone away. "Look, I'm going to give you a pass this one time. Because I've been there and a broken heart sucks. But tomorrow night, in Nashville, you need to suck it up and get yourself together. Okay?"

Her hand flew to her chest without her even meaning for it to. Was her heart broken? Dull ache? Check. Sickening stomach-plummeting feeling every time she thought about his hateful words on the phone? Check. Dizziness and nausea when she considered the many horrific things that could've happened between him and Gretchen when he was drunk last night? Check. Okay, maybe Mia was onto something.

She felt the corners of her mouth turning down. "I don't want to be this girl," she choked out over the lump in her throat. The sympathy in Mia's eyes was too much so she closed her own.

"Shh, I know. I know you don't. Just go back to the bus and get some rest."

"How did this happen to me?" Suddenly it seemed like Mia had all the answers.

The brunette bit her lip and nodded to someone over Kylie's head. "You fell in love. Love is a mean bastard. That's precisely why I avoid it."

She would've laughed if it weren't such a painful truth. "I don't know if he's in love back, you know? Maybe it's just me."

Mia sighed. "I have to go on stage. Like now. But listen, I doubt he would've been all that upset last night if he didn't care about you. Hell, anyone with a pair of eyes can tell he cares about you. But sometimes that's just not enough." The girl's intense gaze met hers. She stared hard for a second as if she wanted to make sure her words were getting through. "You need to ask yourself how important this relationship really is to you. Because from what I've seen these past few months, loving Trace Corbin might cost you your career. Your dream."

She sucked in a sharp breath. It stabbed at her already aching chest. "I can't argue with that, which is saying something." She tried to force a laugh, but with the knot wedged in her throat, it came out sounding strange. "But I don't know if I can let him go. In fact, I'm almost positive I can't. I tried once before."

Mia sighed and cocked her head. "Why not? I mean, what's so great about him? Really?"

She closed her eyes for a moment as she contemplated her answer. He wasn't perfect. But neither was she. She almost smiled as she pictured herself in his arms in Macon. "You know that feeling, when you've had the worst day of your life and it seems like the universe is out to get you? And then you get home and as soon as you walk through the door it's like you're shutting all of that out? The heavens smile on you and you get all cozy in the tub or bed or whatever and all that bad stuff just melts away? 'Cause you're in your safe place?"

Kylie opened her eyes and watched as Mia's brow scrunched in response. "Yeah? So?"

Tears clouded her vision. "That's what being with Trace is for me."

CHAPTER Thirty

It was as if his internal clock was programmed to her. He knew exactly when it was seven and she'd be taking the stage. She'd be looking for him. Expecting to see him in the crowd. She wasn't even mad at him anymore. Her two dozen voicemails said as much. But he was. He was downright fucking furious at himself.

He was going to miss her last show. Not because he wanted to. More like because he had to. If he went there, if he saw her up on stage, he'd talk himself out of what he'd decided. What he'd promised Gretchen and what he knew he had to do.

Walking into The Rum Room was damn near painful. But this was where it had started, so this was where it should end. He didn't see the owner anywhere, for which he was grateful. He wasn't in the mood for talking. Not any more than necessary anyways. He skirted the dance floor and lowered himself into the private booth in the back. It took ten minutes for a waitress to come take his drink order. Thankfully it wasn't the friend of Kylie's who worked there. He ordered his bourbon from the perky bottle blonde and waited for the angry call to come.

Glancing up at the wall beside him he saw the picture of

them on stage the first night they'd met. Seeing her lit up like that, knowing he'd been what made her feel alive that night, was a sucker punch to the gut. Because after that night, he'd been the one to drag her back down. The media outlets were having a field day dissecting her bombed show last night. Drug use, illness, and pregnancy had all been mentioned. He didn't have to speculate on the cause. He knew exactly what her problem was. *Him.*

He was on his fourth drink when his phone finally lit up with her face. Or it might've been his fifth. He wasn't in the mood to count. God, he loved that face. It was slightly blurry. Maybe his screen needed wiping off.

"Hey."

"Trace? Where are you? Is everything okay?" She didn't even sound mad. She sounded…worried. Concerned. He didn't deserve her. He never had. He emptied his glass, savoring the burn as it went down.

"I'm at The Rum Room, Kylie Lou. Can you come meet me? We need to talk."

"I'll be right there." Panic rushed her words out. He wanted to tell her to take her time. Not to get there too soon because he needed more time.

The waitress sat another glass down. This was supposed to be to take the edge off. A farewell drink or two. Oh well. He was going down. Might as well go down in flames of fucking glory.

He pulled off the trucker hat he was wearing and sat it on the table. His full glass of bourbon sat untouched in front of him. He'd tried. He'd tried so damn hard. But every day was like being forced over a cliff and having to dig his way back to the top with his fingernails. Every. Damn. Day. He couldn't do this on his own. Not long term. So when Gretchen had said she was ready to get help, he'd known deep down she wasn't the only one.

He had to save Kylie from himself before he took her down with him. She was about to break out and be huge. It was already happening. She was already on the radio, in the tabloids, and a local well-known. Soon she'd be nationally well-known and then global probably. But not if she didn't unhitch herself from him.

Before it was too late.

He felt her presence before he actually saw her.

"Trace?" Her voice shook with the promise of tears. "What's going on?"

He looked up at his pretty girl. She had on the same red dress she'd worn on their date. He loved that dress. Loved the girl in it even more. Knew she loved him too, loved him enough to let him rake her through the murky pit of hell he was about to drag himself through. "Sit." He nodded at the seat across from him, watching her every move as she slid into it.

He wrapped his hands around his glass.

"You've been drinking," she said quietly. The band began warming up on stage, and between that and the ringing in his ears, he could barely hear her.

"Yeah. I have." He cleared his throat and looked up into her wide blue eyes. Mistake. Her pain was pouring straight out of them.

"Okay, well let's go back to my place and we can call Dr. Reynolds."

"I already called him."

"Oh."

"Sorry I missed your show." He really wanted to down the drink in front of him. But he couldn't bring himself to do it in front of her. He was already about to hurt her bad enough as it was.

"It's okay." Now her eyes held a sadness that made him sick of himself.

"No, it's not."

"Trace, right now, I don't give a damn about the show. The tour's over. Right now I'm worried about you. Please talk to me. What did Dr. Reynolds say?" She was practically pleading with him. This from a girl who didn't beg. *This is what you reduce her to.* He didn't want to drag this out. But saying what he had to felt like plunging his own fist into his chest and yanking his heart out with his bare hands.

"I've got some….*things* I need to deal with. On my own. Alone." He squeezed his eyes shut, but not quick enough. Not before he saw the shadow that passed across her face.

"Trace, what are you talking about? Did I do something? I don't underst—"

"No. Stop, just stop. Just let me get this out, okay?"

She nodded.

"When I saw those pictures of you and Steven—"

"Oh my God." She huffed out a breath. "Seriously? If you would've answered your phone, I would've told you we were—"

"For fuck's sakes, Kylie. Just listen for once in your damned life." He wanted to hit something. He grabbed the glass and downed its contents in one swallow.

"I'm listening," she whispered, her eyes going even wider at the sight of him becoming belligerent. *Yeah, this is me. Be glad you're getting out while you still can.*

He exhaled harshly through his nose. "Those pictures made me think. Not that I necessarily want you with Steve, but at least he's not a drunk. If he says he'll be at your show, he'll be there. Me, not so much." He forced himself to shrug like missing her show wasn't that important to him. Even though it was the absolute worst thing he'd ever done. Which was saying something. Letting her down was the one thing he never wanted to do. And yet, he was pretty sure this was only the beginning. Unless he came clean. Now. "See, I can't promise you shit, Kylie. I can't promise you tomorrow. Or next week, or next month. I never know when I'm going to give in to the urge to drink. I've been fighting it—well, failing at fighting it—for the past few months and I've been miserable."

"You've been miserable?" Her voice was small and it quivered over the last word. Shit. She thought *she'd* made him miserable.

He didn't know how to explain what he actually meant so he rushed on. "It's just been…harder than I expected. And frankly, I'm doing you a favor. You deserve better than this. I'm checking into a rehab facility in Dallas. Tonight."

She took a deep breath and he thought he saw relief on her face. "Oh, well, okay. Babe, if that's what you need to do, then I completely understand. Surely the label will realize that—"

"I don't give a fuck about the label. That's not why I'm doing this. I just…need to work on me right now. And you need to concentrate on your music, on your career. Do you understand what I'm saying to you?"

She shook her head. "Are you…breaking up with me?"

The pain in her voice was too much. He signaled the waitress for another as the band began blaring out a song about a woman loving her man as much as Jesus did. Excellent timing. Nothing like a song about unconditional love while you shattered someone's heart to hell and back. "We went on one date, Kylie. I don't think I have to *break up* with you."

"Don't do this." Her bottom lip trembled. Damn. He should've kissed her one more time first. Long and hard and deep so he'd have the memory to hold on to.

"You're young. All of your dreams are about to come true. You don't need to be linked to me while the media—"

"I don't give a fuck about the media," she said, throwing his words back at him full force.

"Settle down," he said as the waitress approached with his drink.

Kylie whipped her head to the side and glared at the blonde. "Do not bring another goddamned drink to this table or I will tell Clive to fire your ass right this minute." The woman's face went slack, and she turned and walked away with his drink.

He shook his head. She couldn't spend her life saving him from himself. "Listen, I know—"

"Please don't do this. This isn't you. You don't mean any of this. You've been drinking. Tomorrow, when you wake up, you'll—"

"Be in a rehab facility in Dallas. That's what I'm trying to tell you. Move on with your life, Kylie Lou. Enjoy being nineteen. Enjoy making it big in country music like you've always dreamed of doing. Don't think about me or worry about me. I can't have a phone or a computer so it's not like we'd be able to keep in touch."

"But there'll be visiting days and stuff, right?" Tears filled her eyes. He felt like he was drowning in the deep blue pools.

"I don't know and I don't care. I don't want you visiting me in fucking rehab. I don't want them posting pictures all over the damned Internet about you and your loser boyfriend."

"Since when do we care what they say?"

"Since this." He pulled out the two squares of paper he'd folded and put in his pocket. One was a picture of her and Steven. He had his arm around her and they were smiling. The other was from the night he'd nearly been arrested. It was grainy, probably taken by a cell phone. But anyone could see she was upset as the bouncer restrained him just after he'd punched the asshole that had grabbed her in Charlotte.

She glanced at the pictures and shook her head. "You're making a big deal out of nothing. We're just friends. This was taken out of context. You of all people know how the media manipulates everything."

He nearly growled in frustration. She was so damned stubborn. He loved that about her. But right now it was making this nearly impossible. "The label is going to have to cancel the remainder of the tour. They won't drop me right away but it's coming. They won't sign you if you're linked to me since I'm fucking up their whole world right about now."

"Y-you can't know that for sure."

"It's over, okay? Whatever this was, it's run its course and I have to handle me now. I can't do that while trying to do whatever it is we've been doing." The lie burned in his mouth. He could ask her to wait. To wait for him to get his act together. But who knew how long that would be? He loved her too damn much to ask for that. He didn't deserve her. Not like he was.

Her eyes narrowed. "So you're just getting drunk and making decisions for the both of us now?"

"I didn't *just* decide this, okay?"

"How long?"

Trace took a deep breath, causing an ache to spread deep in his chest when her sweet honey vanilla scent hit him. "What do you mean, how long? How long have I known I was going to go into rehab or how long do I think I'll be there?"

She closed her eyes for a second, heartache flashing in them when she stared back at him. "When did you decide this? About rehab, about ending things?" She pulled her trembling lower lip with her teeth and he nearly lost himself staring at her mouth.

"That night in Georgia Gretchen and I talked. I didn't realize—"

"Did you sleep with her?" she asked, hurt filling her eyes as quickly as the tears she wiped furiously away before they could fall.

"Jesus fucking Christ. We're back here again?"

"Did you?" The normally bright blue of her eyes had faded. Washed away by pain. *Because of me.*

"I didn't sleep with Mia or Cora. You can't assume I sleep with every woman I mee—"

"You're not answering my question."

He sighed, barely resisting the urge to reach out and comfort her. Her pain was raw and right on the surface. And he was about to make it so much worse. But he couldn't lie anymore. Not about this at least. "A long time ago. Before you. Before I was anyone."

"You were always someone," she said softly, dropping her gaze to the table.

"Look, I didn't tell you before because this was new and I didn't want to upset you. I wanted you to focus on your career and your success and not worry. Nothing happened with Gretchen. Not this time."

"Except you were honest with her while you were lying to me. I asked you, Trace. More than once. If you were drinking again. You lied."

He nodded. She was right. He didn't know how to explain it in a way that wouldn't cut her even deeper. He could be honest with Gretchen because she was just as screwed up as he was. Plus he didn't give a fuck if Gretchen found out he was a pathetic alcoholic loser and never wanted to see him again. Kylie feeling that way on the other hand...would destroy him. Was destroying him.

"So then why are you here? Drinking and...doing *this*, if nothing happened?"

"Because something did happen. Not with Gretchen, but with me. I can't do this, Kylie. I can't be in a place where I'm going to fall off the fucking wagon every time there's an article or a picture or a—"

She winced. Literally winced like he'd punched her in the face. "So it's my fault, then? I'm the reason you—" She was losing it. Her bottom lip quivered again and she placed her hand over her mouth to cover it.

He barely held back from slamming his fist into the table. Or the wall. Or that damned picture of them mocking him from above. "No. That's not what I'm saying." He raked both hands through his hair. "It just needs to be over right now. I don't know what's going to happen. Shit, I wish I did. But I don't. So just let it go, okay? It's for the best right now." He slid his hat back on, pulling the bill down low so she wouldn't see the moisture gathering in his own eyes.

"You don't mean this." She sniffled loudly. "I don't believe you." The tears she'd been holding at bay finally fell. He clamped his hands down onto his seat to keep from reaching out to wipe them. Images of them together in Nashville, in Macon, in Jackson, in Atlanta forced themselves to the forefront of his mind. Before he could say anything, she made a request he wasn't expecting.

"Dance with me."

"What?" He wouldn't have been more surprised if she'd said, "Marry me."

"I love this song. Just…dance with me. Please? And then if you still want to go…" She lifted her shoulder and let it drop in defeat before she slid out of the booth.

He closed his eyes and shook his head. He'd never be able to say no to this woman. That's what she'd become in the few short months on the road. He didn't know if it was him or the touring that had changed her. He stared at her as she stood there. Vulnerable and needing him. She wasn't a bright-eyed girl anymore. Wasn't his girl. But he could do this one thing for her.

She led him to a back corner of the dance floor and pressed herself against him. Instinctually his arms wrapped around her as they swayed to the damned song that he'd cursed as soon as it had begun. It was the worst he'd ever felt with her in his arms. This close he could feel the steady tremble, the vibration caused by her fighting off the pain and the tears. He squeezed her tight as the song ended and inhaled her warm, sweet scent one last time.

He wanted to kiss her more than he wanted air. More than he'd ever wanted a drink in his life. Wanted to grab her up and take her back to Georgia and just make love to her until nothing else mattered. But he'd tried that method. She couldn't babysit him forever. She had a life, a career, friends. She deserved so much better. He was going to make sure she got it. He just wished it could've been him. Part of him hoped one day it would be him. But today was damn sure not that day.

He stepped back to leave, knowing Pauly was out back waiting to take him to the airport to catch his flight to Dallas. But before he did, he leaned over to kiss her on top of the head. It was the closest he could allow himself to get to kissing her goodbye. "I'm sorry, Kylie Lou."

EPILOGUE

The knocking felt like a fist hammering her skull. Over and over and over. She was lying on her couch in her sweats watching a muted television. Well…not really watching it. On the coffee table sat the latest issue of *Country Weekly* open to the two-page spread she'd read so many times she'd memorized it.

LAST YEAR'S COUNTRY MUSIC ARTIST OF THE YEAR TRACE CORBIN ENTERS REHAB…AND HE'S NOT ALONE.

The pictures of him and Gretchen getting out of a black SUV Kylie didn't recognize were blurry, but it was very clearly them. The one of him holding Gretchen's hand as they passed through the doors was the clearest of them all. They both wore dark sunglasses but there was no mistaking them. Trace had glanced back at the last second, looked over his shoulder—probably suspecting someone was watching.

Yeah, I see you.

Time to work on himself her ass. He'd told the truth about rehab but conveniently left out the part about him and Gretchen checking in together. He'd chosen someone else. Someone who understood what he was going through when she couldn't. Plain and simple.

A deep, dark ache she was becoming familiar with stirred inside of her as the knocking continued. *Is this all for publicity? Rehab? Gretchen? Was our entire relationship for publicity?*

She'd gone so long without eating or sleeping that the reality of the whole situation was blurring before her eyes. *Did I ever mean anything to him? Was it all in my head?* He'd told her once that it was. She didn't believe him then. She did now.

"Kylie, open the damned door or I swear to Christ I will call the fire department!" Now, along with the constant skull-hammering knocking, there was shouting. Fanfuckingtastic. She closed her eyes, pulling the pillow over her head to block out the world. It was a shitty, cruel world anyways, and she was sick of it. She'd tried. She really had. But she was done now.

She'd learned an important lesson though. If you give everything you have to other people and they don't have anything to give you in return…you end up with nothing. Not a single thing.

She'd given Trace Corbin all of herself. Every single thing she had. Her body. Her heart. Her soul. All he could give her was a kiss on the head and a weak-ass apology. And he'd walked away. Left her alone to deal just like her father had.

"I got it," she heard someone say just before a loud click alerted her that the door had been opened.

"Jesus," a muffled voice said. It came from behind her. Kylie rolled over and looked up into four worried faces. Two of the people worked for her. Chaz, her manager, and Maude, her new agent… well, for now. She was also Trace's agent, and Kylie didn't want to be associated with anyone linked to him in any way. Which was why she wasn't answering his sisters' texts or calls. Well, that and she had absolutely nothing to say. To anyone. The other two people in her apartment were Mia Montgomery and Steven Blythe. What the hell they were doing here, Kylie had no idea. She mentally kicked herself for not locking the damned bolt latch. She'd have to remember that in the future.

"Go away." She rolled over so her back was to them. She wasn't on tour, wasn't scheduled for studio time, and didn't have any more phone interviews with radio stations that she knew of. She'd done everything that had been asked of her. Now she just wanted to be left the hell alone.

"Kylie, you need to get up, sweetie."

Mia "I don't even fucking like you" Montgomery calling her sweetie did make her look back. The sympathy in Mia's face set off the deep pang in her chest she was getting used to. She'd seen the article, too, then.

Kylie sat up, hugging her pillow to her and watching them eye her warily, as if she were a cornered animal about to jump up and attack. Or flee for her life. She didn't have the energy for either. "Okay, I'm up." Her voice was weak and scratchy. She couldn't remember the last time she'd said a full sentence out loud. Her mouth tasted like she'd been eating raw sewage for a week.

"Good news," Chaz piped up with way too much pep in his voice.

She cut her eyes in his direction. "I can hardly wait." She would've forced a smile. But she just…couldn't. She couldn't make her eyes or her face or her body do much of anything.

"So, Maude got a special package for you this morning!" He bravely took a step closer. "And we knew you weren't, um, feeling well. So we brought it over."

Her eyelids were heavy and sore from all the crying. It felt like someone was trying to push her eyeballs out of her head from the inside. She was getting a headache trying to keep them open. Sighing loudly, she closed them for a second. "Okay. What is it?"

"It's from Capital, Kylie," Maude informed her. "Capital Letter Records wants to sign you. They're going to take care of the album, the publicity, everything. This is it, what we've been waiting for."

She opened her eyes. All she could do was stare at them as the words tried to break through the thick fog surrounding her mind.

"Come on, Kylie. Say something," Chaz pleaded.

She looked at the packet Maude held out. "Wow. Yay, " she sing-songed softly. She tried to smile. She really did. But her mouth was dead set against it.

"Jesus Christ." Mia shook her head and began giving orders. "Steven, go get a pizza or some of those subs from that Italian deli down the street."

He shot Kylie a sad smile. "Congratulations, Ryans. You deserve this." He nodded at her and turned to leave. His words twisted in her head. *You deserve this. You deserve to hurt like this. You were never good enough for him. It's your fault he had to go into rehab. He never loved you. That's why he never said he did. He's with her now.* She swallowed and tried to nod back. That wasn't what he meant. He meant the recording contract. She closed her eyes again.

"Call me when you've signed them all and I'll take them to Capital. They're already planning your signing party so, um, maybe take a shower and go shopping." Maude set the thick stack of paper down on the coffee table, covering the magazine that lay open. She was a no-bullshit kind of lady—this Kylie knew and respected. So she wasn't surprised when the woman shook her head and left without saying goodbye. Like everyone else had.

Chaz leaned over and kissed her on top of the head. The familiar gesture sliced into her and she winced. "It's going to be okay, sweetheart. Get some rest. Call me soon so we can talk about what's next, okay?"

She went through the exhausting steps of telling her lungs to breathe, her heart to beat, and her head to nod. People got nervous when you went catatonic. She didn't need or want any more unnecessary attention.

After Chaz left, it was just her and Mia. The girl stood in the middle of Kylie's living room. "You're a mess, you know that?"

"Thanks for noticing." Her throat was so tight from lack of use it hurt to swallow. She hugged her pillow and curled onto her side.

"Are you kidding me right now?" Mia's eyes bulged as stepped closer. "You just got a signing offer from the biggest damned label in Nashville. I know you, Kylie. I know how hard you worked for this."

"Lots of people work hard, Mia. Doesn't mean we always get what we want." She understood what he meant now.

"This is effing ridiculous. Seriously. You're pissing me slap off. If Trace needed to go into rehab, then good for him. If he chose to be with that train-wreck of a woman who doesn't have half your talent or drive, then fuck him. But *this* isn't about *him*." Mia gestured at the papers on the table.

His name was a sledgehammer to her heart. But Kylie didn't flinch. She just took it. Welcomed the pain even. At least it was something.

"Don't do this," Mia pleaded, lowering herself onto the coffee table across from her, sliding the contract to the side as she did so. "Don't give it all up, everything you've dreamed of, worked for. Not for this. Not for him."

Kylie clutched her pillow tighter. "You don't understand."

"No, *you* don't understand. This is a once-in-a-lifetime deal. Shit happens. Life is tough. But you're stronger than this. Or you damn well better be."

Kylie shook her head. "I tried to be. I tried to—"

"You tried to what, Oklahoma? Tried to make a name for yourself and now you have so you're going to throw it in the fucking garbage? I know that sounds harsh, and maybe it is. Maybe I'm being unfair to you because…" Now it was Mia's turn to shake her head. Her gaze began to drift off somewhere else, but Kylie was losing her patience.

"Because why?"

"How much did Trace tell you about me?" Mia asked, catching her off guard.

"Nothing really."

Mia took a deep breath and glanced down at her hands. "I'll start at the beginning then."

"The beginning of what?" Kylie breathed in as deeply as she could stand. She really just wanted the woman to leave her the hell alone already.

"How I got here, to American Idol, then on the tour…and why I kind of hate you most of the time."

"Awesome. Can't wait to hear it," Kylie deadpanned.

Mia shot her a sad smile. It was the first time Kylie noticed how vulnerable she seemed. Vulnerable was not an adjective she ever thought she'd use to describe Mia Montgomery. "I didn't grow up in a great situation." Kylie realized she'd been holding her breath so she let it out slowly as Mia continued. "My mom ran off when I was just a baby and my dad was…not a good man. As in, he makes Lily's dad look like a saint. When I was three, he went to jail for beating a man nearly to death in a bar. He's still there. My grandma raised me. My mom's mom. We didn't have much. Sometimes people from the church helped out, made sure we had food and that I had clothes to wear…but it was…rough."

"Jesus," Kylie said softly. Okay, this was not what she'd been expecting. At all.

Mia shrugged and took another deep breath. "My gran and me saved every penny we could to afford my plane ticket to LA to try out for American Idol. When I won, I thought I'd made it, you know?"

Kylie nodded.

"But it wasn't like that. I could only do the things allowed in my contract, and the gigs I wanted to take weren't permitted. The tour with Trace was supposed to be what launched my career, but everyone hated me. I mean *hated* me."

Yeah, she had heard about her getting booed, and she knew first hand how badly that could hurt. "Bet that was tough to take," was all she could think to say.

"Yeah, it was." Mia's eyes went dim. "My gran died two weeks into the tour. I'd just been booed off stage when Trace found me crying on the bus. He said some things I needed to hear but didn't want to."

"Sorry about your grandma." Kylie really was sorry. She knew exactly what it was like when someone died on you, taking your whole world with them. "What did he say?" she whispered, hoping it wouldn't kill her to hear that he'd kissed Mia or something to make her feel better.

Mia shrugged. "Just that I needed to take a step back, deal with my Gran's death, and work on my sound. I couldn't sing a pop cover, then a country cover, then an original song of mine that no one knew all in the same set. And I couldn't keep letting the way other people felt about me reduce me to a sobbing mess of a human being every time things didn't go my way."

She didn't know whether to smile or cry. Sometimes Trace could be pretty amazing. Like he was with his sisters. Like he was with her. "He's not perfect but he's... he *was* something special. To me, anyways," she finished with a slight lift of her shoulder, shrugging as if the permanent lump in her throat wasn't choking her to death. She didn't want to talk about him too much or the missing him would tear another jagged hole into her heart. "You ended up on the tour, so things worked out. Right?"

"I'm getting to that." Mia's eyes narrowed and Kylie sensed that something bad was coming. Something that might be worse than her own pain. Or damn close to it. "After burying my gran and breaking my contract with Idol for personal reasons, which obviously started a ton of rumors, I was broke. Not like surviving-on-Ramen-noodles broke, like lost-the-house, living-in-the-car broke."

"Seriously?"

"Seriously," Mia answered. "I did some things I'm not proud of to get by. And I did get by. I even got a manager finally who helped me get a job cleaning hotel rooms at a place that let me rent a room for cheap."

The pain in Mia's usually strong, steady voice was rattling Kylie's nerves. Hard. She'd thought she'd had it rough, but her life was a walk in the park compared to what Mia was describing. "Mia, I'm sorry you had to—"

The woman across from her waved a hand, cutting her off. "That's not the point. I'm not looking for your sympathy, Oklahoma. The point is I finally got an audition with the Vitamin Water people about the Road Trip tour. And then my manager called and said they'd picked me. And that if it went well, I'd probably get a record deal. I hadn't eaten anything other than the pizza I'd been living off of for a week, and I had literally eleven dollars and forty cents to my name." Her voice was thick, and Kylie felt tears welling in her own eyes. "I thought I'd finally made it, you know? That I'd be okay and that my gran was watching over me and it was all going to work out."

Kylie nodded her understanding. She'd felt the same way when she'd finally got hired at the Rum Room when she was broke and about to be homeless.

"But then a week later I got a call saying they were very sorry to have to tell me, but a new up-and-comer had been chosen instead. They were going in a different direction. *Your direction*," she finished.

The bottom of Kylie's stomach gave out and the room began to spin. She sat up straight and tried to steady herself. "Oh shit. Mia. I swear to God, I didn't know it was you." Her hand rose to her mouth. Probably to hold back the bile rising up from her stomach.

"Right," the other woman said, raking her eyes over her as she spoke. "So you didn't contact Trace about rushing to record that song you guys wrote together so the Vitamin Water people would pick you instead? Because you saw me with him at your party and got jealous?"

Panicked shame made her head throb. She shook her head and tried to concentrate on answering. "No. I mean, yes, I did go see Trace about that song. A lot was going on and we had to talk and I—"

"It doesn't matter," Mia interrupted. "What matters is you got your way, right? You got them to scrap me and go with you. Luckily Lauryn McCray got pregnant and I was offered the spot she left open."

"Mia…" Kylie wanted to reach out, to hug the girl, apologize. Maybe even beg for forgiveness. But Mia stood, obviously ready for this mushy over-share to end.

"Forget it. It is what it is. And even if you had known, would you have done anything differently?"

She wanted to say yes, of course. She would've demanded the Vitamin Water people take both of them if she'd known what Mia had been going through. But she was as hungry for this as anyone else. There wasn't much she wouldn't do to get it. Back then, anyways. Now a part of her wished she'd stayed as far from Nashville as she could have. But she wasn't a liar. "I don't know," she answered honestly. "But I want you to know it wasn't personal.

I had no idea it was you they'd picked." She felt like she was being pounded on by the anger in Mia's eyes. "You don't have to believe me, but I swear. All I knew was they'd picked someone else and recording that song was the only way to make them choose me." *Oh God.* That song. It could come on the radio at any time. Kylie made a mental note to stay the hell away from all radios.

Mia didn't say anything, but Kylie thought she saw the fiery rage in her eyes cool a bit. They were the same. Both of them willing to do whatever it took to make it. Something resembling understanding passed between them. She knew they might never be friends, but somehow they weren't enemies anymore.

She took a deep breath. Being hollow was a weird feeling. She felt as if she could breathe in forever and never get enough air. Mia continued to glare and Kylie sighed. She'd used up all the energy she'd had left. "I don't know what you want from me. Just go tell Capital you'll take my place. Then we'll be even."

Recoiling like she'd been slapped, Mia's expression ignited like she was thinking about *doing* some slapping. "I just signed with Electrick Records, thank you very much. Missed you at my signing party, by the way."

"Congratulations."

"Okay, I get it. You don't want to talk. I'll leave the food in your fridge for whenever you snap out of this pity coma you're in."

Kylie could see disgust and disappointment in her stare but she couldn't bring herself to give two shits about what Mia or anyone else thought. She'd been tough. Been the strong one for long enough. She'd taken everything life had thrown at her and done the best she could to come out tougher on the other side. But enough was enough.

Mia turned her back and began making her way to the door. She stopped before reaching it. "Can I ask you something?"

"Long as you close the blinds and turn the lights off first."

With an audible huff, she did as Kylie requested. "Kylie...what do you think your daddy would say to you right now?"

Well that was a cheap shot. Mia couldn't know, but it just so happened to be the one-year anniversary of her father's death. She wasn't just grieving for the loss of one man she'd loved. She was grieving the loss of both of them. "Get out."

Mia didn't budge. "I will. Soon as you answer the question. How do you think he'd feel about this? About you pissing your dreams away over a man?"

The numbness she'd been mercifully blanketed in began to pitch and roll in waves, pulling back ever so slightly to reveal the exposed nerves. It felt like Mia was tearing her skin off and poking at the wound. "I think it doesn't matter what he'd say. He's dead."

"You don't get off on a technicality, Oklahoma. Your daddy is your daddy."

"Oh yeah? What would you know about daddies, Mia? When was the last time you saw yours?" This time Kylie did wince. She didn't enjoy causing other people pain. She just wanted to be left alone. Was that so much to ask? She was grateful for the darkness so she wouldn't see Mia's hurt expression. "Crap. I'm sorry. I didn't mean that."

"S'okay. It's true, right? But here's what I do know." Light filled the room as Mia flipped on the lights and crossed the floor to yank the shades back up. "I know this isn't you. This isn't the Kylie Ryans I spent the last few months with. So get your ass up and work on getting over it. Before you wake up and realize you have nothing left."

The tears came then. Hot and wet down her face and onto her pillow.

Too late.

About the Author

Caisey Quinn lives in Birmingham, Alabama with her husband, daughter, and other assorted animals. She is the author of several New Adult Romance novels featuring country girls finding love in unexpected places. She is currently working on *Girl in Love*, the third and final book in the Kylie Ryans series. You can find her online at www.caiseyquinnwrites.com.

THANK YOU
Acknowledgements

What an amazing journey book two in the Kylie Ryans series has been for me. I couldn't have ever finished this book without the help of some seriously fantastic individuals.

First of all, I have to thank each and every single blogger, reviewer, reader, and fellow author who contacted me via email, Twitter, Facebook, or GoodReads, to say they loved *Girl with Guitar*. Your encouragement inspires me to keep doing what I do every day. You are my support, my friends, and have become my family. Sorry, you're stuck with me now. My Gutter Girls, Tessa, Erica, and Ashley, you are my A-Team and I could cry all over myself just thinking about what your friendship means to me. Thank you for beta reading this one and for promising to be my bodyguards when the threats of physical violence came. Totally taking y'all up on that.

I can't even say enough about the sheer appreciation I have for people like Julie at A Tale of Many Reviews, Casey Peeler at Hardcover Therapy, Mickey at I'm a Book Shark, Kristy at Book Addict Mumma, Beth at The Indie Bookshelf, Laura at Between the Pages, Lindi at Inspiration for Creation, Stephanie, Kelly, and Tricia at Romance Addict Book Blog, and all of you who work so tirelessly to promote books and authors like myself. You don't get nearly enough recognition for what you do and I am so grateful to have such wonderfully talented and generous people in my corner. Big hugs to my dear sweet proofreader Rahab who has eyes like a hawk and a big ol' heart. I will send you all the country boys I got, girl.

To my critique partners, writing buddies, and fellow Love Junkies, Emily Tippetts, Elizabeth Lee, Anna Cruise, Rachel Brookes, Diane Alberts, and Rachel Harris, thank you all so much for your encouragement, friendship, honesty, and support. And for the emails that resemble therapy sessions so much that you should charge me. I couldn't do this without you. I've learned so much from all of you and am blessed to call you my friends.

Speaking of Emily Tippetts, probably every book I ever publish will have a love letter to her in it because without her there'd be no Kylie Ryans series. She not only designs the covers and formats the books but she is the one who said "you have to publish this" way back when I had no idea what I was doing. (Not that I necessarily do now, but I'm learning y'all). Thank you, Emily, for reading my hideous first drafts and for your endless support of this series. For everything you do to contribute to and improve the writing community. You are a truly special and wonderful human being. I've said it before, but if I live to be one hundred, I'll never be able to really repay you.

To Dominique—my dear sweet Puff, and Ashley Haid, thank you for Tweets that made sweet tea shoot out my nose and for allowing me to quote you both. This book is better because of both of you.

I have to thank my precious husband who is the hardest working man I know and who gives up what little bit of off time he has to be both mommy and daddy so that I can write. To my angel of a daughter who tolerates the many hours on end that I spend with my laptop instead of her and who has informed me she'll allow mommy to work as long as I use the money to take her to where Mickey and Minnie live. Working on it, sweetie. Promise.

To those of you who have allowed me and Kylie and Trace into your homes, your eReaders, your secret Facebook groups, and your lives, THANK YOU SO MUCH. You will forever have a part of my heart. Those of you who participate in cover reveals, blog tours, release week events, and all the many things I ask of you without expecting anything in return, you are truly precious to me. I would squeeze you all entirely too hard if I could reach you.

To Tyler Farr, Hannah Moon, Steven Waldon, and the many musicians and talented management professionals who answered my bazillion questions about touring and the music industry, bless you for your patience with me. You are all rock stars in my eyes.

I have to say one last I heart your faces to each and every one of you who promised to stick this journey out even though this book probably just shattered your heart into a million pieces. I promise I'll put it back together again as soon as humanly possible.

Big smothery hugs to those of you who purchase the Kylie Ryans books during their release week. All sales profits from that week go to The Red Cross for Oklahoma Disaster Relief and I would never in a million years be able to give such a sizeable donation without y'all.

Lastly, thank you to Casey Beathard and Monty Criswell for writing *Like Jesus Does* and to Eric Church for recoding it. Y'all have no idea who I am and probably never will, but your song changed my life and added something truly special to the ending of this book. It has become the theme song to my marriage, though I can hardly listen to it right now because it provokes an emotional breakdown of epic proportions, but it is the most beautiful testament to unconditional love I've ever heard.

I probably forgot to name a few phenomenal people who have done amazing things for me that I didn't deserve, so to those of you, I apologize. I'm a flawed individual with a scrambled, sleep-deprived brain and you deserve better. Please accept this as my heartfelt apology and appreciation.

SNEAK PEEK OF

GIRL IN *Love*

"Thank y'all for coming. I know I'm not great company lately." Kylie looked down at the glass of champagne she held instead of up into the eyes of the guests of her birthday party. The surprise party Mia and Lulu had thrown her. Biting her lip she gathered the courage to glance up. It had been nine months, nearly a year, since he'd walked out of her life. But she was still a shell of the person she used to be. She hid it well enough, or at least she hoped she did. She had two, well, technically three, hit songs to show for it. But the people in this room knew better. And she knew they knew.

The two scheming hosts, plus Carmen and her fiancé, Lily, Steven, and the guys in his band all looked at her with similar expressions. Pity. God she hated that look.

"You've been working so hard lately, you deserved a night of fun." Lulu nudged her shoulder. "You did have fun, didn't you?"

"Yeah, I did. It was great." She forced the biggest smile she could. Lulu's eyes narrowed as she silently called *bullshit*.

"Hey, we should head out. Let you get some rest for your big day tomorrow." Mia threw her a knowing look. Kylie thanked her with her eyes. Of all people, she never would've expected Mia to become the person who pulled her out of her own personal hell these past few months. But tomorrow wasn't something she necessarily wanted to be reminded of. *The Other Side of Me* had gone platinum and the label was throwing a party. One she had no desire to go to. Not that she had a choice.

"I'll walk you home, Mia," Chris, Steven's band's lead singer, offered. Kylie's eyes darted back and forth between Mia, Chris, and Steven. Steven's face remained blank but she saw the slight tension stiffen shoulders. Now there was a weird little love triangle she was kind of curious about. She grinned to herself as she considered nicknaming Mia Yoko.

"We should get going, too. Our flight leaves early in the morning," Carmen said, pulling Kylie into a side-arm hug before walking to the door with her man. "You comin,' Lu?"

Kylie had told them all they could stay in her new place. It was big enough, that was for sure. But they'd insisted on getting hotel rooms. She had a feeling she knew why. She spent nearly every waking minute either writing or in the studio. She knew her weirdo behavior made people uncomfortable, and she didn't miss the looks they shot each other when she zoned out and missed an entire conversation. But she had no idea how to help it.

"Um, nah. I'll get a cab later. I'm going to stay and help clean up."

"Don't be silly. You did all this work and you've had a long trip. I can handle it." Kylie gave her friend a lingering hug and whispered "thank you," in her ear. She hugged everyone else goodbye as they left. Well, everyone except Steven who was still leaning on the bar in her kitchen. Part of her was glad he'd stayed behind. And part of her was nervous as to why. She didn't mind cleaning up by herself. In fact, she preferred being alone. No smiles to fake or forced conversations. But sometimes being alone was…lonely.

Once they were gone, she turned back to the dark haired, tattoo-covered man in her kitchen. "I'm staying to help clean up. Like it or not, Ryans."

She laughed. "Okay, *Blythe*." They worked in comfortable silence for a few minutes, clearing beer bottles and washing dishes left over from the after party portion of the celebration.

"I'll take this out to the dumpster." Steven pulled the big black garbage bag from its can in her pantry.

"Thanks."

She was bent over, putting the remaining unopened bottles of alcohol into her fridge when he retuned. The clearing of his throat startled her and she jumped, nearly slamming her head into the top of the stainless steel door. "God, you scared me."

He gave her a wicked grin, provoking a twisting sensation all through her insides. "Feel free to call me God anytime, Ryans. Or moan *oh God* like the other night."

Her eyes went wide and she slapped him lightly on the chest as he came closer. "I thought we weren't ever going to mention that again?"

He responded with a cocky smirk that was as annoying as it was a turn on. "Who's mentioning it?"

Her chest rose and fell rapidly as he came closer into her personal space. "Y-you are. I think."

"Do you want me to stop?" He leaned in, the force of his bright blue eyes pressing her back against the fridge as he braced both arms on either side of her head. "Say the word and I will."

She knew she should say it. Should tell him it was a mistake the other night, and would be a mistake now. She didn't love him. Couldn't love him. Couldn't love anyone since she didn't have enough of a heart left to love with. But that was what made it so tempting. He didn't love her either. It was just comfort. Trace had up and walked out of her life. Mia had rejected him. They'd found a way to ease the pain. Together. But she felt like hell afterwards. Like she'd cheated on Trace. Or like she'd betrayed herself somehow.

But with him this close she couldn't think straight. She closed her eyes and she still saw it. The source of her pain. Trace and Gretchen Gibson holding hands as they entered a rehab facility in Dallas. Hugging in a hotel doorway in Georgia. Arms wrapped around each other in a parking lot at a bar in Charlotte where he'd supposedly come to see her. They'd been blurry photos online and in the tabloids, but the images in her mind were crystal clear.

She licked her lips, knowing Steven could make them go away, even if it was just for a little while. "Same deal as before?"

"If that's what you want."

She sucked in a lungful of air. He smelled so damn good. Sharp and sweet all at once. A hint of men's cologne and sugary icing from her birthday cake. "I want—"

She was interrupted by a harsh knock on her door. Well that was frustrating. She smiled at the irritated look on Steven's face. "Wonder which one of them forgot something?"

"I'm kicking their ass, whoever it is."

She giggled as they both headed for the door. "It might be

Lulu, and when she threatens to junk punch you, she's completely serious."

Steven growled as they reached the door.

She laughed again. It was kind of nice being with him. Easy. "Consider yourself warned," she told him with a grin.

But when she opened the door with him close behind her, the smile dropped straight off her face. Her world pitched hard left and then right as she completely lost her center of gravity. A bright bouquet of peachy pink roses, held by the last person on earth she expected to see, greeted her.

Emotions she'd held back for so long slammed into her like punches from a prizefighter. "W-what are you doing here?"

His hair was longer and what had once been stubble was a beard. But it was him. If she'd thought his hazel eyes had been stormy before, they were currently a tsunami of colors swirling and threatening to drown her that very second.

"Just wanted to wish you a happy birthday, Kylie Lou."

This paperback interior was designed and formatted by

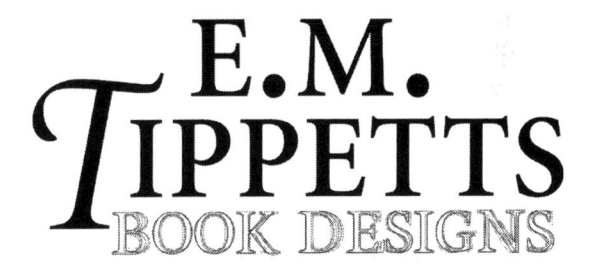

E.M. Tippetts Book Designs

www.emtippettsbookdesigns.com

Artisan interiors for discerning authors and publishers.

Made in the USA
Middletown, DE
16 April 2017